MW00412543

2

7/5

raVine

AND OTHER STORIES

THE ROCK SPRING COLLECTION OF JAPANESE LITERATURE

YOSHIKICHI FURUI

raVine

AND OTHER STORIES

Translated from the Japanese
by Meredith McKinney

Stone Bridge Press • *Berkeley, California*

PUBLISHED BY
Stone Bridge Press, P.O. Box 8208, Berkeley, CA 94707
TEL 510-524-8732 • FAX 510-524-8711 • E-MAIL sbp@stonebridge.com

For correspondence, updates, and further information about this and other
Stone Bridge Press books, contact Stone Bridge Press online at www.stonebridge.com.

Publication of this book was generously supported by a grant from the Japan Foundation.

Originally published in Japan as *Tani* ("Ravine"), *Aihara* ("Grief Field"), *Sendo-ju*
("The Bellwether"), and *Nakayama-zaka* ("On Nakayama Hill").

"Grief Field" first appeared in *Voices* (National Library of Australia).

All stories copyright © Yoshikichi Furui.

English translation copyright © 1997 Meredith McKinney.

Book design by Peter Goodman.

All rights reserved.

No part of this book may be reproduced in any form without permission from the publisher.

Printed in the United States of America.

10   9   8   7   6   5   4   3   2   1

LIBRARY OF CONGRESS CATALOGING-IN-PUBLICATION DATA
Furui, Yoshikichi, 1937–.
    [Short stories. English. Selections.]
    Ravine, and other stories / Yoshikichi Furui; translated from the Japanese by
  Meredith McKinney.
        p. cm.
        Contents: Ravine (Tani)—Grief field (Aihara)—The bellwether (Sendo-ju)—
  On Nakayama Hill (Nakayama-zaka)
        ISBN 1-880656-29-9 (pbk.)
        I. McKinney, Meredith. II. Title
  PL850.R74A25   1997
  895.6'35—dc21   97-5234
                                                                   CIP

Contents

Foreword

YOSHIKICHI FURUI WAS born in 1937 and in 1970 resigned his post as assistant professor of German literature at Rikkyo University in Tokyo to devote himself full-time to his career as a writer. In the following year his place in the literary world became assured with the publication of the novella *Yoko*, which was awarded the prestigious Akutagawa Prize.

Since then, Furui has had an almost cult following among his readers in Japan. He is an acknowledged master of the exploration of that "other" world which lies at the periphery of our "normal" reality as individuals, and his work inhabits the ambiguous borders of these two worlds. His writing likewise often stretches the conventional limits of language, investing words with an aura of added significance that at times lifts his work toward the domain of poetry. The intensity and power of his writing creates an extraordinary realm of experience that the reader comes to inhabit as completely as the bewildered protagonists. All Furui's works in some way circle in toward this same point from new and shifting perspectives, and the cumulative effect of reading them is the experience of being drawn in to explore ever more deeply the strange world that shadows and defines our normal waking life.

Of the four works collected here, three are stories and one, "The Bellwether," is a somewhat more discursive and essayistic treatment of a theme, weaving in elements of the Japanese *zuihitsu* (essay) and I-novel traditions. "The Bellwether" is from Furui's earliest collection, in 1974, and was written soon after his return to Tokyo following several years spent teaching German literature at Kanazawa University in western Japan. "Grief Field" was first published in 1976, and "Ravine" appeared in 1980. "On Nakayama Hill" won the coveted Kawabata Yasunari Prize in 1987.

Meredith McKinney
Kyoto, Japan

Ravine

DEEP IN THE MOUNTAINS there is a voice, chanting holy sutras. Drawn by the sanctity of its timbre he wanders among the mountains, seeking, but the owner of the voice is nowhere to be found. When he returns half a year later, the voice is still faintly audible. This time he conducts a thorough search and discovers, at the bottom of a ravine, the meager whitened bones of a man who had hung himself from the cliff above by a hemp rope tied around his legs. A further three years pass, and still the chanting has not ceased. Marveling, he this time carefully investigates the skeleton and discovers that the tongue inside the skull remains unrotted, and is even now continuing to chant with unwavering devotion.

Lying rolled in my sleeping bag in the darkness of the little hiker's hut in the ravine, I recalled this old story of the uncanny voice that rose with the sound of the rushing water from the valley floor, a story I had heard in the classroom a good seventeen or eighteen years earlier and forgotten till that moment. It came back to me now, as a chill autumn rain came racing suddenly in from the mountain, beating at the branches of the forest, and shrouded the ravine where I lay in a sound that merged with the sound of the stream's rushing, till it was as if the rain was pouring upward, out of the earth. And it seemed to me then that, from beneath the almost paralyzed quietness that lay wrapped at the heart of the water's roar, the rich and lustrous weight of a chanting voice reverberated with an astonishing clarity. When I listened intently, there was in fact no single voice discernible. But now it seemed to me that the tumble of water noise in the ravine had instead begun to swell with the breaths of many different people.

This was not the first time I had been bedeviled by auditory hallucinations in the mountains. Once, for instance, at the end of autumn on a night wild with wind and rain, I had heard the midsummer song of a cicada. From deep in the forest there emerged that sharp and numbing shrill, and it echoed back also in layer upon layer from the opposite wall of the ravine. The more closely I listened, the clearer it sounded. It must have been caused by a sort of buzzing in the head due to extreme fatigue, but I could not distinguish it from the sounds of the outside world except for the fact that, when I tried raising my head, it abruptly ceased. I believed for a long time that this auditory hallucination was peculiar to myself. But in the hospital just before he died, Koike confided to me that he too had often been troubled by the cry of cicadas in the middle of the night when he was in the mountains. Nakamura also said he could remember such experiences. Though we three had frequently gone into the mountains together in our twenties, this was the first time this had ever been mentioned among us. . . .

Nakamura, lying next to me in his sleeping bag, moved restlessly from time to time and emitted something between a sigh and a groan. He had struck his lower back against a rock that day as we walked, and the pain was apparently still with him in sleep. It was mid-October; the traditional service of the forty-ninth day after death had now passed, and—in memory of the man who, until the morning he finally lost consciousness, had spoken constantly of our mountain walks together—we were performing what could be called a memorial climb for Koike. It had been five years since our last mountain trip together, when we were thirty, and for both of us the lack of any real exercise in the intervening years had caused drastic physical changes. Until that spring, Koike had also lamented his paunch whenever we met, but when I saw him again three months later he had grown thinner than he had been in his twenties. After fifty days of hospitalization he had finally died at the end of summer, his body parched dark with suffering, leaving behind a wife and two children of five and three. Stomach cancer had taken him at this early age.

Thinking about it now, I realized that from our earliest plans for this memorial climb we were swept along on a strange wave of elation at being the survivors of our companion's death. It was almost as if the chill breath of our dead friend were brushing against us. There was an excited lift to our step; we seemed both physically and mentally to regain our youth, and we were somehow entranced with the sense that we, at least, could still climb mountains. We had met up whenever we could in the midst of our heavy work schedules and briskly accomplished the task of planning the trip, each privately fearing that his physical strength might not be up to it, and somewhat ashamed at the precipitate and unrealistic nature of the decision, given that we were men in our mid-thirties, each with a family; and now here we were actually in the mountains, with a climbing schedule such as we used to set ourselves in our twenties, and an equivalent weight of equipment on our backs. The previous day, the first day of the walk, we had indeed felt the effects of our lack of physical training. We had exhausted our fund of energy simply in carrying the rucksacks from the foot of the mountain up the ravine as far as this hut, so that on our arrival it was all we could do to prepare and eat the evening meal, and we rolled into our sleeping bags leaving the dirty plates to lie as they were on the earth floor, laughingly agreeing together over a cup of sake that after all we needn't feel we had to go all the way to the summit tomorrow if this present exhaustion were still with us in the morning. But in the morning we had woken refreshed and had been impatient to be off as we ate breakfast and cleared up. Slinging a light knapsack over our shoulders, we began to climb through the sweet morning scent of the conifer forest, at first gingerly testing our strength, then gradually growing almost ecstatic at how wonderfully firmly we were walking, each familiar motion and each new mountain view bringing back memories for us, until after four hours of drunkenly joyous climbing we found ourselves effortlessly arriving at the summit.

On the way back down, the threat of rain in the sky hastened our steps, and when we reached a rock scree, Nakamura suddenly lost his footing. His foot slipped only slightly on the loose rocks, but he tipped over backward and didn't try to twist around to save himself from falling; instead he continued to slide down a good fifteen feet, his astonished eyes fixed on my face till finally he rolled over onto his side and came to a halt, striking his lower back against a rock with a dull thud. It wasn't a particularly dangerous situation, but it gave me a rather nasty feeling to see Nakamura, who was usually a man of more than average agility, so suddenly passive and unresisting.

"It's not that I was taken by surprise," he explained in bewilderment when he had scrambled back up to where I waited, "it's just that, purely and simply, my body didn't try to save itself."

When night came the ravine suddenly grew chill and a

cold rain came rushing incessantly downstream off the mountain we had climbed that day. Night in the ravine differed from the experience of night on a flat plain: even inside the hut, hearing did not function so much horizontally as vertically. One moment the stream's sound would be heard echoing upward into the sky, and the next instant something would shift so that it seemed now instead to be pouring down from above. The wind carried in the swelling sea song of the conifer forest up on the ridge, came beating down on the corrugated iron roof of the hut, and passed on into the ravine beyond, and then in a kind of reverse wave the sound of creaking branches came thrusting back up from the path of the wind. Only the weight of the darkness sank ever more intensely. Finally the rain squall swept everything to oneness within its roar, passed over, and was gone, and now in the sudden silence that pierced to the very quick of the skull, one's own consciousness seemed like a tiny yellow light shining meaninglessly in the huge depths of the mountain darkness.

When we had cleared up after the evening meal and sat warming ourselves by the embers, drinking whiskey and dreamily breathing in the fragrant smoke, Nakamura complained that his lower back hurt. We had a joking exchange about it. At our age backache was merely a humorous complaint. The talk turned naturally to the question of our sexuality now that we were reaching middle age. We were in the midst of some licentious talk on the subject when Nakamura suddenly stretched his back and winced, then grinned through the wince. Taking the fact that the fire had died as our cue, we spread our sleeping bags side by side on the wooden platform and lay down, pulling the hoods up over our heads so that only our faces were exposed to the now rapidly chilling air, and spoke for a while of the dead Koike. Our talk became somewhat oppressive.

"The worst thing about going to see him in the hospital was that he kept wanting to touch my body," Nakamura murmured, already drowsy. "He'd suddenly stare at my arm or my chest while I was talking, and then his thin hand would come sliding out toward it. And he'd just keep touching it, with a kind of envious expression. That would have been back during those hot summer days. . . ."

The conversation had grown rather grim, and we stopped talking. The same thing had happened to me many times with Koike. It wasn't so much that he envied our health as that he marveled at it. He would fix his eyes on me intently, as though staring at something incomprehensible—something he couldn't believe without touching it. Finding myself gazed at thus, sometimes stroked by his thin weak hand, I had constantly to fight down an almost unconquerable sense of idiot arrogance at my own survival, a sheer joy at the fact that I wasn't in Koike's place. Nor was that my greatest unkindness toward Koike.

"I'm putting it out," I said to Nakamura, and blew out the candle. The hut was immediately soaked deep in the sounds of the ravine. The faint light that still hung even in the darkness of this night now slowly spread a gray swathe across the floor from the small window, making the plates and water bottles and rucksacks stand out blackly around our bed. Whenever Nakamura twisted his back and groaned, I teased him with a low chuckle, and he laughed grimly back. After some time of this, Nakamura suddenly lifted his head from the sleeping bag and turned an intrepid face toward the door.

"Isn't that someone coming up the ravine?"

The squall had just stopped, and nothing was audible except the sound of the stream, and the occasional fall of a branch.

"Must be my ears," he said lightly, and lay back and began again the low moaning at regular long intervals, until eventually he no longer responded to my chuckle but seemed to have fallen asleep without his moans ceasing. I found then that I seemed to have taken over the role of sentinel. I couldn't manage to get to sleep. To induce myself, I imagined the sleep of a timid animal. The instant it hears a sound that has some meaning for it, deep sleep becomes complete alertness. For this to happen, it must first be thoroughly asleep. It's impossible to have that instantaneous reaction to a sound if you hear it through a wakeful doze. The eyes spring open, and it makes a hairsbreadth escaping leap aside from the claws of death. Then, once it has escaped to temporary safety, it immediately falls asleep again, oblivi-

ous to the screams of its companions. There is no consciousness of having been saved.

I was beginning to doze off with these thoughts when,
from farther down the ravine, I heard the forced breathing
of someone climbing a steep slope with a heavy weight on
his back. The climber's hot, uncontrollable panting, which
seemed to be retching out his very heart with each gasp, was
clearly audible in the lulls between the expressionless
rustlings of the trees. No sooner did it seem to have approached somewhat than it merged with the stream's sound
and disappeared. Then, after a long time had passed, it was
there again at just the point it had been before. I had many
times had the experience of welcoming a climber who
arrived late at night at a mountain hut. Climbers generally
follow the principle of avoiding unnecessary intimacy with
members of another climbing party, but when someone
comes in very late he generally receives a carefully casual
welcome from the unknown companions in the hut. They
emerge half asleep from their sleeping bags, pretending they
just happened to have woken, to stir up the now-dead fire
and warm the remains of their dinner for him, sometimes
sitting up half the night with him in desultory talk. No, the
footsteps were coming no closer.

Then for a while the events occurred within a dream. I
sank to sleep with my ears still straining to hear. As I slept, I
could still distinctly hear the sound of the stream and Nakamura's moans. In the distance, what could have been an

owl's cry stood out as a single point within the hollow darkness. Suddenly the footsteps rapidly approached and came to a halt outside the hut. Nakamura and I lifted our heads at the same moment. The man was having difficulty opening the door from the outside. We went to lend our strength from within and then, suddenly, a tall man had crossed the threshold and stood in the hut gazing blankly about. A single glance told us that he'd lost his way in the dark and spent a long time wandering out there. Nakamura went round behind him and released him from his rucksack, and I stood in front of him to help him off with his anorak. Just at that moment the man opened his eyes and mouth wide, uttered a voiceless cry, and slumped forward against me, and as he clasped my chest with both arms his body began to convulse. I staggered backward holding him, and managed to sit down on the edge of the raised wooden platform behind me, to sustain his weight; then I braced my legs and heaved his sturdy body up. When the two of us had finally succeeded in laying him down between our sleeping bags, his face was already that of a dead man.

"He's dead," we agreed with a hastily exchanged glance, and in a panic we set about trying to revive him. Nakamura knelt beside him, stripped back the sodden shirt and undershirt, and began to rub his blue chest fiercely with a dry towel. I quickly gathered firewood and lit the fire and, for some reason, set about boiling some water in the cauldron. But as fast as we worked, just as rapidly did his appearance transform itself. Nakamura's massaging did not produce even the faintest flush on the man's chest, and when Nakamura began to work up onto the neck, his movements pushed the man's head so it lolled over sideways, and from the mouth and nose now turned toward me, dark clotting blood flowed.

"Come on, let's sleep," said Nakamura, tossing the towel to the floor; he hastily scrambled feet first into the sleeping bag beside the corpse and immediately set up the same regular moaning as before.

We lay there under the weight of the darkness, with the dead man between us. Whenever Nakamura moaned I had the illusion that it was the dead man, and turned to Nakamura to say, "Hey, he's still alive." And each time I did so, that blue face with its bloody nose and mouth laughed straight in my face. Beside me the corpse had the heavy cold weight of an object, and I felt it sinking interminably farther and farther down into the blackness, on its face an eternal grin of somehow mocking agony. The weight of it was being precariously suspended there between our combined breathing on either side. If we once relaxed our strength, the sinking corpse would pull us under with it. I was astonished at the quiet will at work in the very act of breathing. Then suddenly it seemed the roof and the floor had been removed, and we were floating free in space above the ravine, with the corpse slung between us. The sound of the flowing water connected directly with the expressionless weight of the corpse, and the soughing of the branches was now the sound of the monstrous expanse of time itself. In all that ravine, only we spread around ourselves a tiny warmth, within which we lived. I searched the water sounds desperately for the sound of another person—let it be a voice or footfall, a moan, a gasp, even a last dying cry, as long as it somehow, ever so slightly, shook the expressionlessness of the ravine.

And then a chill rain began to fall, and the ravine began to seethe again, and I awoke with the sound of sutra chanting in my ears, and a sense of having been saved.

It must have been the voice of the sutras that Nakamura and I had heard chanted countless times in the interval between Koike's wake and the forty-ninth-day ceremony for the dead, which had sunk deep into my ears and now returned to me as a voice from the depths of the ravine. Yet the voice sounded so vividly human. It was a rich, ponderous voice, almost as if the human flesh itself had been tempered till it rang. It seemed, I thought, like a sound made in imitation of what one would imagine to be the sanctity of the first sound uttered from the silence of one newly dead. Straining my ears, I felt it was still implicit in the sounds of the stream—so indistinguishable from that natural water sound, yet so distinguishably a human voice, with the echo of every human passion within it.

The rain passed over and the ravine returned to a deep quietness, with only the constant sound of the stream. But the quality of that quietness was irrevocably altered for me.

From every corner of the ravine's darkness that wrapped me round, there now swelled intimations of all the breathings of the human flesh, which wove a thick silence all about me. There was even the suggestion of the trembling voice of a woman. Of course the only sounds that actually existed were the groans of Nakamura close beside me and my own breathing, and all these other sounds were no more real than the cicada's song on that stormy night, the effect of my small life force pulsing softly in the eardrum or in the capillaries of the inner ear, which merely made deceptive imitation of the countless lives in that vast darkness beyond. Yet it was nevertheless the motion of life, and saying this to myself I called before my mind the image of Koike lying motionless on his hospital bed. . . .

EVEN AFTER ALL SIGNS OF consciousness had ceased, Koike remained as a merely physical existence, and for two hours more he continued to groan. His wife called Nakamura and me into the hospital room, and we stood against the wall, watching over him, helpless in the face of his suffering. When Koike's breathing had stopped and the doctors had left, Mrs. Koike gently wiped her husband's forehead with a handkerchief, then put the handkerchief to her own eyes and drew a deep sigh. At that moment, the sounds of the distant street came surging into the sickroom. A soft sobbing flowed within the sounds. I didn't so much hear this sound with my ears as greedily gulp it down into my cold chest. Cocooned in the survivor's sense of reprieve, I had not the wherewithal then to grieve at the death of my friend. Nakamura too was leaning heavily against the wall, face up and eyes closed, his shoulders heaving roughly, as though he had just managed to come through a difficult rock climb.

The deep sighing of a woman welled up in the darkness. The white swelling of the throat was implicit everywhere in the dark, unknotting and smoothing the stiffness of death. There was something in the sound that was akin to the sutra-chanting voice. Even the soft creaks of branches in the wind had about them a hint of woman. All the sounds in the world came whispering enticingly in with the sighing, like the soft rustle of clothing in a voiceless room.

As the voice of my dead friend's wife, needless to say it smote my conscience, but it was at the same time some other woman's voice. Koike had also heard that voice. He seemed indeed to keep the enticement of this voice before him right up until the moment of his death. . . . In the early autumn of the year we turned twenty, we three made a rare visit to the seaside. At midday we lay together in the pampas grass of a broad hill that extended out as a promontory above the sea, our bodies soaking up the warm heavy rays of the sun, unable quite to adjust ourselves to the leisurely pace of existence here compared with our trips to the mountains. As we lay there we talked about women, we who as yet knew nothing of them.

Suddenly from the bushes nearby there welled up the sound of a woman's heavy dark panting.

Then followed a gasping cry, naked with painful physicality. We three sat up simultaneously and gazed in the direction of the voice. After a moment, a woman in a white dress emerged onto the road from the shadow of the nearby bushes and came walking past us with long leisurely strides, heel and toe, her arms folded down low on her belly, her back serenely straight. She headed into the sea breeze, half turning to send a vague glance in our direction as she passed, then was hidden again in the shadow of the bushes farther along the road. She appeared somewhat older than we were. It was difficult to imagine how that heavy panting of a moment before could have emanated from such a gaunt body. A tight black belt bit into her waist, and a straw hat hid her face from forehead to nose in deep shadow, with slightly parted lips and a thin pointed chin poking out below it into the sunlight. It was only the chin and lips that seemed to be turned on us briefly; the eyes gazed vaguely at some distant point far beyond our heads. Her neck, arms, and calves were white and lusterless, and the surrounding brightness made them appear somehow clouded and opaque.

We waited for the excitement that the panting had aroused in our bodies to recede, then got to our feet. When we emerged and set off after her, the woman was already far ahead along the gently winding road, on the point of disappearing into the pampas grass. Once we reached there, we had no idea where she had gone, so we stood stock-still, bathed in the light of sky and sea, feeling helplessly that something more ought to have come of this. I blinked slowly in the sunlight. When I closed my eyes my body seemed a soft transparent red, and on opening them, a darkness like heavy oil filled me. The repetition of this was like a listless breathing.

Even Koike's sudden dash into the nearby bushes provoked no more than a dull surprise in me. I turned my gaze in the direction he had gone, and the top half of the woman's body suddenly swam up above the grass heads, her oddly white and pinched profile turned to us, against the black glittering expanse of the sea. The figure was somehow difficult to get into perspective; she could have been a hundred feet or more away. I watched Koike's mad dash toward her with a sensation of pleasure, almost as if it was my own sexual desire that was plunging headlong at her. The woman became aware of the footsteps behind her, turned quickly toward us, then, with a fierce look, disappeared as if sinking backward.

"You mustn't die!" cried Koike, and he too disappeared, his diving body thrusting the grasses aside. Nakamura and I looked at each other in astonishment, then set off after them.

Koike was crouched facing the edge of the cliff, huddled paralyzed like a hunted animal, and tiny shivers ran over his body.

The woman had crossed the low iron railing, and with

an almost graceful movement she sank down right at the cliff edge and slowly pushed her legs over the edge, her hectically flushed face all the while turned on Koike with a steady glare.

"Please don't," Koike pleaded, huddling still lower and slowly inching forward on his knees two or three shuffles at a time, judging the best moment to spring at her.

For a long time they remained staring at each other, waiting to see whose strength of will would win out and break the balance. Nakamura was preparing to make a simple lunge at her from the side, but this seemed a dangerous move to me and I stopped him. Koike was now gradually relaxing his pose, and the woman seemed to be slowly cringing before him.

He had reached a point where a single step would bring him within reach of the railing to which the woman's hand clung, and suddenly he leapt at it. He missed his moment by the merest breath; the woman released her grip on the rail, slipped over the edge of the rock and disappeared, still in a sitting position, pitching forward with her back arched as if shouldering away the sky.

"Wait!" shouted Koike, straddling the railing, and with his left hand he clung to it for balance while he stretched his right hand down over the rock ledge.

Above the rim of the rock the woman's face, her face only, rose up like a white death mask against the glittering sea.

"What is it, honey?" she said to Koike in a thin clear voice. Then her purple lips seemed to smile.

"Please don't," Koike said thickly, and then he sprang away from her, scrambled back over the railing, and came tumbling over to us on all fours. As he did so, the woman turned her face to the sky and disappeared over the edge of the rock. There was a sense of something like a heavy sandbag sliding down the cliff face, then she was launched into the air with a wild scream that was neither man's nor woman's, which trailed off into a long moan, and finally at a dizzying depth her body thudded dully into the water. Koike put his hands on the earth, twisted sideways, and vomited. Then he shook his head violently from side to side, and soundlessly began to cry above the vomit.

I left Koike in Nakamura's care and ran headlong back down the hill to the fishing village in the inlet below. At every turn in the zigzag road I was afflicted with the sensation that the sea's horizon with its dense light was bearing down upon me. I rushed into the little police station and gave the news, but the officers seemed to be quite used to this kind of event; a group of people was quickly assembled, and they set off in a fishing boat from the pier, chatting together about the last time this had happened, and disappeared round the cliff, the motor making little soft explosions as they went. They took with them a net that looked just like a fishing net, saying they would drag the corpse to shore through the water. After a while Nakamura and Koike both arrived, each looking as pale as the other, and we three stood together in silence gazing at the sea.

"They've gone by boat to get her out," is all I said to them.

"I should just have made a dash for her at the beginning without hesitating," said Koike, in a dull voice.

"There's a strong smell of fish around here," Nakamura muttered, squatting down on the seawall, and then he vomited into the sea. The vomit spread out finely through the clear water and sank, and little fish gathered to sip at it, the sides of their bellies flashing.

Thirty minutes later the boat reappeared from the shadow of the cliff. I peered at the stern, but there was no sign of anything being dragged along behind. The men in the boat were smoking sullenly, in a mood quite unlike the one they had set out in. As the boat approached we craned forward with the urge to see what fearful thing could be seen, and there discovered in the bottom of the boat on the pile of brown fishing net a small wet collapsed shape. We could make out a white calf with the veins standing out blue in it, and an oddly elongated nape of a neck, and then two arms cradling a bowed head.

"She's alive," one of the men said to us, a little dejectedly.

We assumed that she would be, at any rate, close to death, or badly hurt at the very least, but when the boat reached the pier and the men called to her, she lifted her head, pulled the wet hair back from her cheeks with both

27

hands, and setting her hair in order stood up sinuously, with a listless air. Once she was helped onto the rock by both arms, she bent slightly forward, took her wet dress in delicate fingertips, and pulled the skirt away from her body, then with eyes modestly cast down to her bare feet, she began to walk off.

"You're not, you're not hurt?" Koike asked in a shrill voice, stepping backward as she walked past him.

"No thank you, I'm quite all right," the woman replied in the same voice we had heard on the cliff edge, and off she walked between the men in the direction of the police station, her head meekly lowered, casting him not so much as a glance. To the children who came running up, she turned an embarrassed smile.

It was then that a cold fear finally gripped me. That body, with its white death mask of a face, which had been sucked out into space leaving in its wake a somehow hollow sound, that body was still alive. Drenched though it was, it now walked through the quiet fishing village looking like a normal woman. It was even smiling kindly at children. The stink of fish suddenly assaulted my nostrils. The bay, with its downpour of sunlight, went dark before my eyes, and the woman's bare feet as they trod the sand grew harsh and vivid. Behind Koike and Nakamura, who stood there in astonishment, watching her go, I squatted in shadow and softly retched.

Since the woman had in the end been unharmed, it

would have been sensible to laugh off our dismay when we recalled it later. This is what we always did after we had emerged from some dangerous situation in the mountains. But, apart from marveling together at the power of her good fortune, we didn't speak further to each other about the event. We got the bus straight back to the town from there and caught the night train home, cutting our trip short by a day. As we sat in the bus, Koike muttered, "You know, it really is a weakness in us, not to have any way of praying in this sort of situation. It means that you end up bearing the brunt of everything yourself, even the things that are too much to bear."

"Well yes, maybe," Nakamura replied. "But when I saw her stand up in the boat back there, I just thought 'Praise be!' That's all I thought. But I think really that was a kind of prayer."

I was about to say what suddenly came into my mind at this, that if I were to pray to anything it would be to the awe-inspiring nature of that woman, that it's to fearful things that one prays; but at the strange image that this idea conjured up I lost my nerve, and I said nothing.

To the end there was a deep reluctance among the three of us to bring up the subject of that day's events. When Nakamura and I were alone together, we did speculate on the nature of this woman about whom we had learned absolutely nothing, on her reasons for suicide, and what might have become of her subsequently. But when with

Koike we never spoke of the event. Koike had become a man who could no longer look women in the eye.

It was Nakamura and I who together threw ourselves into bringing this woman-shy Koike together with the woman who subsequently became his wife. Watching frustratedly from the sidelines, misgivings filled us as we saw our friend only flee the more as the attraction grew. It had been our early obtuseness there by the seaside that had put Koike in the position of facing the terror of that event alone. While Nakamura and I had gone on to have for the most part unproblematic relationships with women, Koike alone had been unable in any way to shake off the aftereffects of the event, right into his thirties. Our sense of our own responsibility in this weighed on us. Also, we were feeling somewhat threatened by Koike's lover, the woman who later became his wife. She had become exasperated at how he would dodge aside at the last minute, just when he'd seemed to be reaching for her, and she finally demanded that he introduce her to his best friends so that she could learn more about him and come to terms with things a bit; she got from him the names and workplaces of Nakamura and myself, and one day she telephoned me. Koike had told me firmly that I was to keep out of this, but I could clearly see how attracted he was to her, and when she telephoned me I agreed to go out to meet and talk to her on several occasions. But how could I, who myself couldn't really understand Koike's feelings no matter how he tried to explain them, manage to sound convincing to her on the subject? Her pride as a woman had been hurt by Koike, and she was haggard with the impossibility of parting from him. The more I tried to explain, the more irritable she became, and she plied me with questions for all the world as if rebuking me. In the end it was I who was convinced by her, by the fierceness of her love, which eventually sealed my lips.

One night, when she was yet again firing questions at me, I finally spoke of the events by the seaside. She listened then with her eyes fixed on mine. "And ever since, Koike has been the way he is about women," I finished, with a sense of really providing her for the first time with a worthwhile explanation. But in fact it served only to infuriate her.

"So that's how you men feel about women, is it?" she demanded, and she shifted sideways to look past me and refused to respond to all my attempts to justify myself. After a while I became aware that everyone around us was taking this to be some kind of lover's quarrel, so I urged her to come outside.

As we walked together toward the station, I glanced at the tearful face beside me, quite preoccupied and apparently unaware of whom she was with, and the weird thought stole over me that if I suddenly embraced her now things could develop into a three-way relationship with my friend, and then that this could actually make the lovers' relationship rather more straightforward. It was of course an impossibility. Even without taking Koike into consideration, if I contrived to get myself alone with this woman, who knew how she might attack me for my earlier blunder. After parting from her at the station, I went on to Nakamura's place and told him the story to date, finishing by saying that as things stood I'd done Koike a bad turn, and that I left the next stage in his hands.

A week later he came to see me, looking glum.

"Look at it how you will, Koike's in the wrong," he began, in typical Nakamura style. "He just carries on the whole time about his own feelings, and he's making no attempt to shake off his fears for the sake of the woman he loves. He just doesn't deserve to get her, he isn't qualified as a man." But there was a certain bewilderment behind his words.

We agreed that we must make every effort to bring the two of them together; it never for a moment occurred to us that this could be construed as uncalled-for meddling.

Luckily, Koike's married life appeared to go smoothly. Each time we met, Koike seemed more open and relaxed, and his wife's former raw, nervous quality now became swathed in a plump fleshiness; her skin bloomed and shone. A child was born. Then, with a timing that seemed almost to be putting that marriage's success to some personal test, Nakamura married, followed by myself.

Five days before Koike died, I called at the hospital. It was another of those days of heavy rain, and the sickroom was imbued with a faintly marshy scent of wet rocks and forest humus. Koike sat me down on a chair by his pillow, and his dark emaciated face looked somehow dazzled as it gazed up at me, while he set about recalling in intricate detail an occasion when the three of us had lost our way in a ravine on one of our climbing trips. This event had occurred more than a year after the event beside the seaside. We had taken a wrong turning on a path that we had been along twice before, and headed confidently up a completely unfamiliar ravine.

As we followed the stream up, the valley sides grew steeper, and we scrambled up a succession of rock ledges we had no recollection of having come across on our previous trips—yet still we resisted the conclusion that we'd come the wrong way, and almost perversely chose to continue. Then, just when we reached a point where it seemed the path along the ridge above might be almost within our grasp, we found our way barred by a fair-sized waterfall. It was only when we'd clawed our way up to a ledge halfway up its side, and gazed at the dismal sight of the rock face above, that we began to think seriously about our position. We had arrived at a place that seemed to be the deep innermost recess of the ravine; within our range of vision there was only the waterfall, its endless stream pouring with a kind of uncanny slowness from somewhere above our heads, the black rocks that hemmed us in on four sides like a bowl, and a sky that was rapidly darkening with clouds. We stood in silence for a long time, gazing up at the rock face. It wouldn't be impossible to force our way up it as we had forced our way up so far, but at this point we had simply lost the spirit to attempt it. We were not so much searching for a way up as privately taking the inner measure of just how much spirit each of us had lost. Koike alone was impatient. His opinion was that, in the case of a nasty place like this, it was the least danger-ous option simply to take a deep breath and climb through it without hesitating and that the longer we stood and con-templated it the more our psychological defenses would crumble; he seemed astonishingly unconcerned with the question of whether it was the right path or not. Astonished though I was, I myself was actually still of two minds as to whether we had mistaken the way. After a little while, Nakamura dealt with the question summarily by saying that whatever the case may be, we should retrace our steps to the first fork in the path. Once it was spoken, this seemed the most reasonable option. We went back down the rock face with ropes and returned to the meeting of the two streams in the same amount of time we had taken to come up, then set up our tents there for the night, as the ravine was rapidly darkening. When we emerged from our tents in the morn-ing, it was clear at a glance that we had gone the wrong way at that point. We had turned up a side stream one back from the point where the path branched, and followed it all the way up the ravine that ended in the sheer cliff etched by its waterfall, without noticing our mistake.

"How could we have been so stupid?" Koike demanded

fretfully from his hospital bed, almost as if it had happened just the other day, as if that mistake had led to the gravest of consequences.

"It's all too common with ravines, to make mistakes that seem ridiculous later."

"Yes, but we'd done that walk twice before, hadn't we? You'd think among the three of us someone would have realized instantly that that dismal little ravine wasn't the right one."

He spoke accusingly. Resentment focused his eyes on some distant point in space. Then his right hand emerged trembling from beneath the blankets and took my right wrist in a loose grip. His rough dry palm began stroking my arm repeatedly from wrist to elbow. I swallowed down the disgust that rose in me, and a simultaneous disgust at the sudden consciousness that it produced in me of the greasy sweatiness of my own arm, and replied in a carefully calm voice, "It was because we were tired. We'd walked a long way, remember. When you get tired the brain can't make judgments anymore, you make them with your body: We've walked this far, so this must be the point where we turn off, and so forth. And the tireder you are the sooner . . ."

"You turn up a side path." There was a strangely ironic smile at the corners of his mouth as he spoke. "But then there's no option, really. The darkness inside you makes the whole ravine dark, doesn't it. There's no point saying it was brighter or darker last time we came here. Because each time is the first time. Still, that feeling of going up a ravine you seem to know, or maybe you don't after all, that sensation halfway along that you can't go any farther. . . ."

As he muttered, Koike renewed his grasp on my wrist and drew it under the bedclothes toward his flat chest. My face approached his as he pulled me down, and he gazed into my eyes and lowered his voice to a conspiratorial whisper, as though imparting some important secret. "I've remembered! That cairn—remember? The one where the streams met, a bit out of the way, little heap of five or six small rocks, just piled up as though someone had come along a moment or so earlier and thrown it together in passing. A sign, but from its position you couldn't really tell whether it meant 'go straight ahead' or 'turn left here.' Yes, a treacherous bit of mischief. We'd just come down from the right side of the river; that's why that cairn seemed to be pointing up to the left. But I've remembered now. The moment we went left up that stream I thought, 'This is odd. This is wrong.' You thought the same. You did, didn't you."

"Yes I suppose I did," I replied, unable to avoid supplying the answer he was urging on me; and in fact, now that he mentioned it, I did seem to remember that when we first turned off I had a strong impression that this was wrong, but my feet went tramping on in rhythm with theirs without my having the strength to gainsay the other two.

"We were led astray, that's what it was, just because we didn't pay enough attention at that point where the paths divided." There was a certain urgency in his whispering voice. The core of his eyes seemed to blaze up in a wavering flame. "That's why all we could do was to go on in silence, even when we realized the truth later. That's what it was. But I saw, up on that rock ledge, I saw it, drawing us on from above, peering down at us over the edge there, a woman's face. . . ."

"If you saw a woman's face, why didn't you tell us! What sort of a friend are you?" I tried to lighten the moment with a feeble joke, but as I spoke I found myself pulling my hand and face away from Koike. My tug made Koike's face flop upward from the pillow, and he clutched my arm with both hands. A face that seemed to contain equally both laughter and tears, a face that could have belonged to any of the images one sees surrounding the central Buddha in the dark of temple altars; I knew from the experience of my mother's death that that face had the clear marks of death upon it. A cold confusion of fear gripped me and I rose from the chair. Koike stretched his hands to my chest, gripped my shirt and clung there shaking for a long moment, and a heavy groan thrust itself from deep within him.

"You're both with me, we're always there the three of us when we go into the ravine, you were there too weren't you? You're always the careful and perceptive one, Nakamura can make decisions. . . ."

Mrs. Koike flew in and separated us, pulling Koike's hands from my chest and covering me with her back. She

shot me a glance, signaling with her eyes as she put a fore-
finger softly to her temple, then held Koike against her and
pressed him down onto the bed with her body.

"I don't want to die, not all alone, I don't want to die!"
Koike cried out from beneath his wife's breast. He continued to cry aloud and weep.

His wife put one elbow on the bed, raised herself on her
left leg, turning toward me the almost translucent whiteness
of the back of her knee, lifted her right leg from the floor
and put it on the edge of the bed, and gently pressed her
breast to the upturned face of her weeping husband. Then,
as she stroked his long tangle of hair with her fingertips, she
too began to cry softly.

From within the sound of the rain, a rich sobbing and
moaning swelled and died.

"I don't want to die," Koike groaned several times more,
as if reminding himself, but—strangely—his wife's sobs
seemed to be calming him.

Once his groans had ceased, Mrs. Koike rose from the
bed, quietly straightened the hem of her white dress,
brushed the hair back from her forehead, turned her somewhat flushed face to me and lowered her eyes, and in a
slightly husky voice said, "I do apologize."

Koike's eyes were closed, and he was breathing gently
with sleep.

After my agitation, my mind became a blank, and I just
stood bolt upright against the wall listening to the sound of

the rain. But in the grim face of this death, at that moment when being alive seemed as unbearable as dying, my heart had been strangely touched by the two voices I heard. And it was only now, when the first commemorative ceremony of Koike's death was over, as I lay straining my ears for the sighs and moans of the myriad voices contained within the ravine's sounds all about me, that I at last understood just how my heart had indeed been touched that day.

Grief Field

"I WAS IN A FIELD," MY friend said queerly, "with the wind blowing around me. Just as if I'd never grown up." The grass stood knee-high as far as the eye could see, and long undulations traveled through it, wave upon wave. He was walking slowly before the wind. It was night. No, not yet night, but just when the sun begins to set. The dark, low-hanging clouds were suffused with a purple fire, and only a pale marsh of light still hung between sky and earth; yet his palms showed faintly red, with the thick veins standing out hard in them. His right hand hung open at his side, but the recent sensation of a deathly grip on some weaponlike object still stiffened it. A moment before, he had impulsively flung the thing down into the grass, and now, suddenly, all was calm around him.

His clothes were damp, not from rain, for the rain had not yet come on, but from within. The ground was already sunk in darkness, and as he walked he felt the constant brush of unknown things that lay deep in the grass; but by now he was moving on without the slightest pause or stumble, casually treading down the sinister touch. His body grew heavier with each step he took. But the wind swelled at his back, faded, and swelled into another breath, and the grass bent down in waves which spread out ahead of him, shining white, so that his body too turned a transparent white, became the countless grasses and flowed out with them, on and on over the field, parentless and childless now, freed of people, freed of self. He said that at the time he imagined that this must be how it is for a wild fox when it reverts from the human form it will sometimes take, discards human thought, and dances deep into the grass.

"You must have been dreaming," I responded from time to time, half automatically; my friend simply could not have been in a field of deep grass for those seven days. In the phone calls he made to my house night after night, the din of a barroom was audible. After the second call, his wife phoned me, trying to find him. He hadn't been home for the last two nights, she said. He had been told that he had lung cancer and that his relatively young age meant that it had quickly passed beyond the first stages already. She said bravely that he'd never been one to complain so she was more than willing that he should do whatever he wanted now, he could visit women if he liked, all she wanted was to hear his voice, if only for a moment, to speak just one kind word to him—but she was afraid that if he phoned her neither of them would be able to avoid mentioning his illness.

On the third evening, I was ready for his phone call, and when it came I begged and pleaded with him to tell me where he was, saying that if only he would agree to meet me I would go there immediately, without saying a word to his wife. But the more I urged, the more extraordinary his replies became. He began muttering something about having committed a terrible crime, then suddenly he grew excited and started accusing me: "There you are, calmly going on living, and you ignore the fact that all the while you're murdering people!" Then later that night there came another phone call, in which he rambled on about this and that, his voice completely relaxed, saying that he'd finally calmed down and asking me to tell everyone he'd be home again shortly.

And so it went on. Once he even murmured a couple of lines from an old Buddhist song—"Sad that we see it not, though the Buddha be all about us. . . ."

It was in one of those nightly phone calls that he first told me about being in the dark field, in the wind. After this I returned to bed filled for some reason with a calm certainty that this time he really would go home, but toward dawn I awoke and, though only for one brief moment, I tensed at a new thought, for I suddenly recalled that some ten years before his younger sister had died in a double suicide with her lover. Perhaps he really had killed someone, perhaps he and some woman attempted a double suicide and he had failed to die, and he really was wandering around somewhere.

A day later, in the early morning, my friend returned home. He was in a thoroughly unhinged condition and was hospitalized immediately. The following morning a woman telephoned me. In a tearful voice she explained that he'd given her this number to call in case of an emergency, that for the last week he'd been crazy and she'd been looking after him day and night, but then near dawn the morning before, he'd seemed at last to have grown calm, so she'd relaxed her vigilance and fallen into a deep sleep, only to find when she awoke that he'd slipped out of her apartment; that she'd waited a whole day but he hadn't come back, and she was afraid he'd killed himself. I told her that he was safely at home. "I see," she said softly, and hung up.

"Yes, it must have been a dream," said my friend again with a laugh. "I'm not saying that I have no idea what I did during those seven days. At this stage I may not be able to remember everything that happened, but that doesn't mean I needn't feel responsible for what I did. It wasn't anything so simple as running off to another woman then running back to my wife, rejecting one as the other attracted me. I can't justify anything, but I have to make myself remember exactly—and not just to get things straight, but to take responsibility, you see. . . . "

When I heard these words, coming as they did from a man on his deathbed, I had to look away. On the third day after he was hospitalized he had apparently sat his wife down at his bedside to tell her, in an admonishing tone, that they were to stop hiding the matter from each other, they both knew what was going on, she mustn't say anything, they must be silent on the subject but not from any desire to keep things from each other; and when his wife burst into tears, he lay there stroking her back for a long time. He had already handed her a list of all the instructions he could provide concerning the settlement of his affairs after death. When I was with him, however, he always spoke as if he were finally on the road to recovery after a long illness.

His hair, which showed almost no change from his twenties into his thirties, had suddenly begun to whiten at the temples, and for some reason it now seemed to hang finer and softer. His face had lost its heavy masculinity, and now somehow the features of a girl or an old woman showed through. But beneath the film of enervation, his eyes contained a clear strength.

"There really are such things as 'dangerous years' in your life, as the old tradition has it," he said thoughtfully. My immediate impulse was to retreat from this hazardous topic, but the positive tone of the convalescent never faltered. "No doubt these years take each of us differently," he acknowledged, and then, haltingly, he told me the following.

"From roughly a year ago, with no forewarning, sometimes my body would suddenly be seized by an urgent sense of grief. It wasn't so much an emotion as a physical sensation, almost a stab of pain. I couldn't discover any particular reason for sorrow—goodness knows, the things that had once made me unhappy were too far in the past to affect me now. And it wasn't at all like melancholy, either. It probably sounds odd," he said, "to say that my knees wept silently, that the pit of my stomach sobbed. It's like that almost-fainting sensation that spreads over the body from the center of pain, when for instance you hit your shin on something and hold your breath to control the pain. I've sometimes thought, as a sort of joke, that my soul was trying to break loose and my body was weeping over its own heaviness.

"In the beginning this fit would come on me once every few days, then later it got to be almost every day, until finally it came to the point where it would happen several times a day, regardless of time and place—in the middle of a meeting, say, or when I was having dinner with the wife and kids. It was sometimes such a violent spasm of grief that for a moment I'd be seized with the need to crouch down on the spot. And yet while this was happening, I was at the same time always aware of behaving almost overconscientiously, responding to people almost overscrupulously. I've always been careful to preserve appearances; for me, this has been a way of loving, and I imagine I'll continue to do so. I decided that, even if these attacks kept happening for the rest of my life, I'd never go crying on other people's shoulders. But when this thought crossed my mind, the self who at that moment was perhaps in the middle of a brisk discussion about some complicated work or replying to my children's talk, would seem like a scene from the distant past; and as I reached out toward what was almost a nostalgic memory of myself, something would go slithering down inside my body. And I realized that it was probably this remote self upon which my children relied implicitly.

"I would open my eyes at daybreak and, though there were no tears, I would have the sense that my whole body had finally cried itself into a state of calm. It wasn't so much grief as a feeling akin to nostalgia. A desolate wind came blowing up from the western horizon. When my mother died," he continued, "when I was ten, I saw a hole suddenly appear in the horizon, and for years afterward, every night when I went to bed and every morning when I awoke, on my skin I would feel the passing of a wind that blew from that point. It was still blowing when I reached the age at which the heat of my body had begun to oppress me. My younger sister slept in the bed next to me, breathing always with a high-pitched whistle, the result of the asthma she'd suffered from early childhood."

He was over twenty when his father died, in great pain. His stepmother remarried almost immediately, but within two years she too was dead. On the night he received the news of her death, the hole in the western horizon still gaped open, but the wind had long since ceased to blow. When his sister died with her lover, she too was drawn into that hole, and from it not the slightest sound of the cough he knew so well came back to him. All was silent. Within this silence he married and had children. Because of this silence, he never ceased to feel something miraculous in the sheer ordinariness of family life, he said, and hence never knew the luxury of wearying of its everyday repetitions. . . .

I wondered about that, but kept my question tucked away in one corner of my mind, and maintained my role of attentive listener. I knew a certain amount about his "woman habit." He wasn't a man to play about with women. Again and again he would fall for someone, she would fall for him, they would seem as close as if they'd been bound together by years of love and hate, then after a month or two it would come to an abrupt end. Several of these women had later come to me and asked what had happened to him, as though I were his protector. They were all around thirty, with somber, intelligent-looking eyes and an unconsciously apologetic smile directed at the world; and when I told them what I knew of his former relationships, they didn't get angry but simply nodded sadly. It seemed strange that, though they were obviously attached to him, there was no evidence of their trying to hang on to him once it was over. All these women struck me as being somehow like his wife. No matter how many times he repeated this kind of relationship, it seemed, he neither wearied of the pattern nor varied from it, nor did he ever seem to experience the pain of a broken heart.

"A dangerous year," my friend continued, with that same confident tone of the convalescent, "is a time when one's vital forces are in an even more vulnerable state than in puberty, a time when the membrane of life suddenly grows thin. You interpret this instability as a sign of growing rigidity, you're unprepared for this exposure of your life force, you're left wide open to being invaded by things. During the past two or three years I've shed the final skin of life—and now that I've taken this fatal illness into the core of myself, I'm finally moving into a peaceful old age."

When he came out with this statement, I finally lost any grasp of what could be going on inside him. Was all this cool, disinterested talk in fact a product of his realization that he was close to death—an attempt to quell the fear and envy he felt when faced with someone healthy? Or had he already reached the stage of having transcended his own life and death? Or was it that, though on the surface he appeared calm, inside he was still quite mad; that he had shed from consciousness not only his sense of fear but, together with this, his sense of reality? And now for the first time I began to be leery of the vaguely bewildered smile that constantly hovered on his face. That new whiteness at the roots of his hair, which was the first thing that had struck his wife when he stood in the doorway after those seven days, again came home to me. His rapid breathing was obvious even as he lay there in bed.

During this time, I had a chance to talk to the woman

who had looked after him in her apartment for those seven lost days.

She was true to the pattern—an intelligent-looking girl of a little under thirty, who had been rejected by her provincial family and now lived independently. Her relationship with him had begun two years before, and for two months they met virtually every week either at some outside place or in her room, until quite suddenly, without any forewarning as far as she could see, he ceased to call her. When she called his workplace he would say, in precisely the same tone as she'd heard when they were still meeting, that he was busy this week and would talk to her the following week. Being the sort of person who couldn't chase people, who hated to make someone feel pursued, she limited herself to an occasional phone call just to hear his voice, but it made her suffer to find that he was avoiding her in spite of all the care not to pester him. She began to hate going home to her room with its telephone, and her life in general began to go downhill— even her face underwent a temporary change. Yet, oddly enough, she never really held it against him. Instead, she became miserably convinced that she didn't really understand male-female relations, that she could never really become attached to someone she liked.

This went on for over a year, and then one evening, about the time when she'd begun to regain a certain amount of tranquillity at last, he phoned her to say he was in the area and would it be all right if he stopped by; and after about

thirty minutes he arrived, looking quite exhausted, and settled down contentedly beside her, saying with a sigh, "Ah, I
do feel at home here." She too breathed an internal sigh of
relief and promptly forgot the intervening year. His visits
began to occur regularly once a month. He asked her in
detail about her life. She was a person who rarely spoke
about herself to others, who even privately was almost horri-
fyingly indifferent to her own past, but she was amazed at
the eagerness with which, under his guidance, she set about
describing her life and actually began to like herself as much
as before she had despised herself. He would come in the
early evening, and when one o'clock came would quickly
collect his belongings and leave with the light step of a
young man. She would carefully avoid seeming to cling
when they parted, and would sink into sleep, retaining the
happiness she had felt while he listened to her tales. She
always woke at daybreak, and, lying there watching the
room grow pale, she would have the sensation of her own
face suddenly transformed into something fearful and
demonic; but remembering his voice her features would
relax. Though the phone calls came only once a month, she
hurried home each evening. Previously, standing before the
silent phone, she used suddenly to be overwhelmed by the
painful sensation that her body was actually rotting moment
by moment; but now she found comfort in the waiting.

"I'm aware that there's a lot I should be figuring out,"
she said to me, "but I'm satisfied with the situation as it is—

just knowing that once a month he's fond of me. Anything more, and people begin to frighten me."

Though she was close to thirty she still seemed a young girl, with that kind of youthfulness that goes well with jeans. Her self-effacing words momentarily moved me, and perhaps this was why I felt an anger toward my friend come snaking up inside me. To my knowledge, this was the kind of woman my friend always had his relationships with; or rather, all the women he had a relationship with he changed in this way, by somehow draining the spirit out of them. I recalled his austere way with his own sons, too, and with what solemn tenderness he treated them when they visited him in the hospital, although they were already developing the dignified air of young men. "Isn't he just making you play it his way?" I said to her, disloyal though this was.

She smiled almost tearfully, and gave me a strange reply. "He's always been the sensitive and considerate one. It's me who's insensitive; there's something lacking in the way I perceive people. You know, four years ago I lived with a man for a while. He became dissatisfied with me almost immediately; it was awful to watch his silent misery. Finally he left. You'd imagine that this would have caused me such pain that I would have been afraid even of looking back on that time; yet somehow I ended up just going on living in that same room we'd rented together. I'm still like that—simply indifferent. . . ."

In the beginning it had been she who wheedled my

friend into reluctantly coming to her apartment. He would sit about looking bored while she made drinks for them; but then one night it happened that, when she was standing with her back to him looking for something in the wardrobe, he said abruptly, "I had a younger sister, you know." Then all that night, haltingly, his eyes blind and vacant, he told the story of his sister, who had died at the age of twenty-seven in a suicide pact with a man who left behind him a wife and children. Several months before her death she had suddenly started turning up at her brother's apartment, no doubt driven by the helpless feeling that she was slipping deeper and deeper into an abyss. She never appeared to have anything in particular to discuss, simply hung around trying to be helpful about the house, apparently waiting for him to ask her about herself; but he had his hands full with his own affairs at that time, so he chose to go on ignoring her, and her death had been the conclusion of it. Toward the end she had burst into tears and confessed that she was having a hard time of it with her man, but he had dismissed it, and simply told her that she'd do better to call it off if that was the case.

For her part, the girl said, she was nothing but pleased that he had at last brought out something painful to him, and she stroked and stroked his hair as he sat there like a child, sunk in silence. Though this was in fact their last evening together before he stopped seeing her for a year, it never occurred to her to wonder whether what had happened that night had been the reason for his leaving. On the contrary, she held the memory of that occasion dear as the happiest moment in the two-month relationship.

Coming home late at night, she often found herself thinking that it had been a mistake to have him come to her room. When she opened the door the air would be thick with the scent of her morning rising, and she even sensed, there in the middle of the room, a face swollen with sleep, turning slowly toward her with a frown. For she and this room had almost become a single entity, though she had found it quite by chance and lived there a mere four or five years. At this stage she and the room had so grown together that whatever she might do with whomever and whenever while in the outside world, indeed even were she to do away with herself, her real self was all the while protected safe within these walls. . . .

When he came to her room again after a year's absence, he had only to say "I feel at home here" for the aversion she felt for her own room to disappear completely. He, too, soon ceased to sit around in her room looking bored, and instead began to listen to her with a relaxed attention. One difference in him now was that about once during each visit his whole body would suddenly become stiff and motionless; he appeared to be holding his breath, a cold sweat soaked him, and from time to time it seemed as though a long slow wave passed over him from his chest downward to the pit of his stomach. His eyes were lightly closed. At such times he would give no more than a vague answer no matter what she said to him, so she would simply sit beside him and let herself become absorbed in drawing pictures or writing words with a finger on his chest, which was broad enough normally and now seemed to have grown still larger.

"'For dalliance, for pleasure are we born,'" he suddenly murmured darkly one evening in the middle of such a fit, opening his eyes a fraction and glancing quickly around; and then abruptly he gave a choking laugh. She noticed that his chest was instantly bathed in a cold sweat.

After these episodes he would inevitably proceed to talk of melancholy things, in a bright, almost singing voice.

For example: "You know how a tiny noise can suddenly seem to avalanche in one's head, though it doesn't actually grow any louder? Ever since I was a child, just as I was sinking into sleep or just on waking, I'd hear the trees rustling in the garden, or water flowing, or insects singing by the veranda, or someone coughing, and though all these sounds were soft enough in themselves, suddenly they'd overwhelm me with a violent oppressiveness. Like tumbling down a slope, or finding a locomotive suddenly bearing down on you, or someone suddenly shouting, 'Fire! Run!' You move your arms and legs in the bedding, hear the brush of your own clothes against the sheets, and it's as though the sound all of a sudden takes off and goes rushing out of control, its eyes wide with terror. The voices of your parents casually talking in the next room sound suddenly as though they're fraught with the muttered intensity of a quarrel. Everything continues calmly, and yet it's a sliding avalanche of sound. And in the bed beside me, my sister would always be tossing in some nightmare. . . . "

Or, for example: "Do you ever have times when you keep meeting people you haven't seen for years, running into them? There you are, head bowed even lower than usual perhaps, yet on the street or in a train someone calls your name, and it's a person you haven't seen for five, ten, fifteen years. And it just keeps happening. At first you're elated with the sensation of suddenly finding yourself the center around which the world revolves, but after a while you begin to have the frightening feeling that your past is being mustered up before you, that people may even be gathering from the world beyond. And it's always at those same times, too, that people are constantly mistaking you for someone else, isn't it. They don't call out to you, they come walking up, looking hard at your face. Then they stand there, gazing at you intently with their head cocked to one side, and wait for some change of expression from you. And then there are the friends who say, 'I saw you at X the other day. I thought of calling out, but you seemed in such a hurry,' and you say, 'That's impossible. I wasn't there,' but they won't take no for an answer. And so it goes on. What can it be, do you think? Could it be that somehow the individual frame of who you are temporarily loosens and the pattern of a certain type of face shows through? People who knew you long ago would be more likely to recognize that. They could approach you more easily. Sometimes my present friends say, 'I thought I was mistaking someone else for you at the time, but now I take a look at your face I realize it actually must have been you.' But it really had been someone else. I'd never been in the place when they thought they saw me there. My sister, just before her affair with that man began to drag her under, was terribly afraid of this sort of thing, you know. . . . "

Or, for example: "Have you ever had the kind of nightmare that is completely motionless? There's scenery, but you don't know where the place is, you don't know what the circumstances are, no one's visible, and in fact you aren't even present yourself. That alone is enough to set you crying bitterly. You look up at a tree and feel yourself disappearing into the thickness of the trunk, and you moan aloud with wretchedness. Somewhere far off in the distance lies a completely ordinary stone, and that little stone is somehow connected with your own body, its existence is far heavier and more powerful than your own, and it sucks you in, farther and farther, till you can no longer breathe. Or, it's a winter evening, the leafless branches are trembling and shivering on the tree, and somewhere someone, in a voice wilder than the red evening sky, is bellowing over and over again the same phrase of a stupefyingly dull song. Or, there's a flower in a garden, and it grows larger every moment, and it turns whiter every moment—and then suddenly you realize that it's blackest midnight around you.

"I never talked to my sister about our home or our parents before she died, but one evening as she was squatting in the narrow doorway of the entrance to my apartment preparing to leave, squeezing into her tight new shoes, she said to me, 'Do you remember there used to be a place called Grief Field near our house? Because just the other night I had a dream where I went to a dark field that had that name, and, listen, you remember how when she was sick our mother sometimes used to leave her bed and slip out into the field at the back of the house, didn't she? Well, I was crouching down weeping like she used to there.' 'There was no such place as Grief Field near our house,' I said to her. 'You'd better watch it, you know. You're overstrained.' 'Yes,' she said, 'I'll be careful. But the dream wasn't all bad. I felt as though I was being promised that, once I'd come this far, the rest would be taken care of—that I wasn't alone,' and she looked me in the eye and went out. After she'd gone I could still hear her thin cough far down the road in the cold night."

Always at the end the talk would come around to his dead sister. "But even then," the girl said, "I listened as though he was talking about me, as though he was expressing his love for me. In fact, I felt as if his words were precisely identifying things about myself, as though he'd been watching me ever since I was a child. So when he talked about his sister I took it in as naturally as everything else, and never wondered what might be going on inside him. I'm terrible, I just don't understand how other people feel. I lost my mother early, and he said that's the reason."

So naturally, late that evening, when he knocked on her door and she found him standing there, his features in some way veiled by a thin film, she welcomed him with a little internal dance of joy at the idea that at last he had come because he really wanted to see her. She helped him out of his rain-soaked coat and went into the kitchen to prepare the drinks, so breathless with joy that she had a small fit of coughing. When she came back he glared up at her, a certain suspicion visible in his very posture.

"So you didn't die. You were living here all along. And I've suffered and suffered these ten years"—and he seized her shoulders and burst into tears. A kind of shudder seemed to spread through the room then, almost as though another woman had come walking quietly in. As the girl stood there dazed, rubbing the broad back of this man so much older than herself, she thought "this person's mad," and she felt herself beginning to be sucked into the depths of a bottomless anxiety; but then she was buoyed up by a sudden surge of possessiveness and thought to herself, "Now that he's come here mad, he's mine."

She turned down the light, thinking he probably didn't want to be looked at, took off his clothes, and put him to bed, whereupon he curled up his limbs, still whimpering, and sank into sleep. She snuggled in beside him, rubbing his back, and she too fell asleep. Some time later, a noise woke her, and she opened her eyes to see him taking his jacket off the wall and slipping his arms into it. His tie was neatly tied. It was not yet three a.m.

"Where are you going?" she asked.

"Home," he said briefly.

In the face of such cool composure, she could say nothing; she simply lay and watched him leave. He stooped in the doorway and put on his shoes, presenting to her that solid, masculine, utterly imperturbable back. Then he casually picked up the ladies' umbrella propped against the wall, and a pair of rain shoes, and went out. After a moment during which she simply sat there, her head tilted in surprise, she leapt up, threw a raincoat over her nightgown, and ran out after him.

She first looked anxiously toward the railroad crossing, but it wasn't in that direction that she discovered him. He was quite a long way off, walking fast along the road that led into the new housing development. His figure paused for a moment, then turned the corner purposefully and was gone. She followed him. He was striding along at such a brisk pace that by the time she had finally caught up with him she didn't have breath enough to call out, and he showed no sign of turning to notice her. She thought of trying to walk beside him, but, catching sight of the umbrella gripped firmly in his hand, she suddenly sensed that he was in that state in which he could very well mistake her for the dead again, and she felt that this time she too might get drawn into it, so instead she chose to stay a little behind him, without a word, and keep her eye on him from a safe distance. He turned corner after corner at each crossroad, with every appearance of confidence, leaving the development, going on through fields, through the local wood, then cutting through an apartment house complex, every so often stopping to look left and right as though to regain some memory, but apparently untiring. After a while, however, he began to go around in circles, and when he came to a corner he would stand a long time in thought, or looking up at the second-floor windows of the apartment blocks; until finally, when the sky was growing pale, he sat himself down on a bench in a small park. "Where is it you're going?" she asked, coming up and sitting beside him, and taking the umbrella and rain shoes from him. "I don't know," he said, his head in his hands. Did his hair really have so much white in it? she wondered, startled.

Once she got him home again, he slept on in her bed until evening. She was forced off the bed by his large body and ended up sleeping on the floor. Again and again she was woken by the sound of fearful groaning, each time shaking his shoulders until he grew calm and the sound ceased. Then, at around five, she locked him in the room, still sleeping, and went down to the shop by the station. Hurrying back, she saw as she drew near that he was sitting on the bed with the window of her second-floor room open, gazing down at the street, his large pale face utterly devoid of expression.

He sat on the bed while she moved about the kitchen preparing the evening meal, and his eyes followed her like a child's. When she had placed the meal on the low table he slowly got off the bed, staring at the food with a kind of wonder. Then a shiver seemed to run through him, and he set about eating ravenously. In no time he had finished off food enough for two.

After dinner he said, "Have you got a pack of cards? I'll teach you how to play *koikoi*." She became very cheerful at this and flew off to the nearby stationery store for a pack of the tiny flower-patterned cards. They played with complete absorption long into the night. She didn't ask him about his state of mind, or his home, or his office. As long as things could continue like this, she had no desire to talk about anything that might throw light on what the future had in store. Near midnight, he suggested they go out for a drink, so she took him to the little bar by the station. In the bar he continued to chatter on gaily, and to treat her with his normal easy tenderness. He asked to use the phone and carried on a loud conversation with someone at the other end.

That night, she slept in his arms. Even as she slept, she was aware of the sensation of being gazed at, of being touched on hair and cheek and throat. It was already past nine when she woke, pushed out of bed by him again. "Look what happens when you doze off," she thought with a wry smile, and she took up the telephone and called her workplace with apologies to the effect that she wouldn't be in today either. She had a moment of wondering how long this could continue, even given the easygoing nature of where she worked. She also wondered just what his children were being told back at home, but it was only a passing thought, and she lay down beside the bed and fell pleasantly asleep again. When she next opened her eyes it was near midday, and he was still sleeping. Quietly she cleaned up the room and got breakfast ready, but still he didn't wake. He was sunk in a profound sleep. Sensing something odd, she looked about her. Against the wall at the bottom of the bed his shirt and trousers lay as he had tossed them, and the trousers were wet from the knees down. She went out to the entrance and picked up the men's sandals that she'd bought on impulse at the store the day before, and they too were heavy with moisture. There was no evidence outside of any rain having fallen since the previous evening.

The events of the next five days seemed jumbled together to her later. Every day from dawn to dusk he slept like an animal, from time to time tossing violently in some nightmare. He would bolt down the evening meal voraciously, after which his face would assume an expression of deep contentment. Then he would apologize for all the worry he was causing her; but after a while he grew depressed again, and then he would come out with a strange assertion.

"Actually," he would say, "I killed my sister." He always spoke with so solemn an expression that when he first began saying this she was half inclined to believe him, and she felt a vague apprehension about their own relationship; but when she questioned him a little more closely he produced in almost obstinate detail fragments of his own life at the time, in which he was unaware of his sister's imminent death, and then when she questioned him further he retreated to talking about his childhood.

When the mother died, his little sister had become the favorite of the grandmother on the father's side. This grandmother was one of those religious types who never miss a sermon at the temple, and under her influence the little girl developed a pious manner of talking and a generally lugubrious air. Consequently, the other children disliked her, and persecuted her at every turn, and after her grandmother's death she was always hanging about at her brother's heels. But it was he who was the most brutal of all to her, in fact—whenever he grew the least bit irritable, he would jeer at her, keep on at her till she could no longer speak for wretchedness, then grow angry at her utter subservience, and finally lose all control of himself and set about beating her. Even then his sister only crouched there, with tears dribbling down her cheeks, and never uttered a sound. And when he walked off, she would follow a little way behind, contritely.

One day, on a sudden impulse, he pushed her into the river. Naturally, once she'd surfaced, she gazed at him reproachfully. But she made not a sound. If she'd floundered about a little, she could have reached the bank; if she'd tried to stand, the water would only have reached her chest. Yet she floated passively, face up in the current, her lips forming inaudible words while her face slowly began to sink beneath the surface. Horrified, he ran about fifteen feet downstream along the bank till he found a place that gave him a good foothold, and as she floated by he managed to haul her out. Once out, she sat plump down on the grass, turned to her brother, and clasped her hands before her breast, mumbling some religious-sounding chant. And when they got home, she told them simply that she'd been standing there day-dreaming and a gust of wind had sent her into the river, and she sat out the scolding in silence. She was only seven at the time.

When she visited her brother's apartment for the last time, nine days before she died, she had stood still for a moment before she left and hung her head, as if offering her profile to her brother's gaze. "She's prepared to take any-thing I have to say," he thought, and the old cruelty rose up in him again as he stared at her scrawny neck; but he said nothing. That night he could hear her cough from even far-ther down the street than usual as she made her way back through the night to the station, and when suddenly he ceased to hear it, he had a momentary sensation that she had left the street and passed on to some different place.

"It was I who killed her," he repeated time and again. The woman would nod in response, but she pleaded with him not to be so hard on himself, not to go making himself miserable like this. She even went so far as to say that, life being what it is, one never can tell when doing or failing to do something, speaking or failing to speak, might not be effectively the same as actually killing somebody; but surely one must simply accept this. She found herself watching him narrowly, though. No, he was certainly not giving voice to a guilty conscience—his face was that of one entranced, in the grip of some grotesque delusion. Before she realized it she had begun to argue with him in angry earnest: "You never killed her!" She threw at him one by one the inconsistencies in what he was saying. She mercilessly exposed to him his confusion of fantasy and reality. He rose softly to his feet then, and proceeded to lumber up and down the tiny apartment, between the room and the kitchen, glancing at her maliciously from time to time.

She sat still and erect in the middle of the room, alert, wondering just what was going on, and every time he muttered, "I killed her," she replied sharply, "You didn't!" She spoke from a deep, icy sanity, with neither tenderness nor sympathy. A sanity somehow mad. But after thirty minutes, faced with this man who simply continued to pace her room, oblivious, a deep mental and physical exhaustion slowly began to overwhelm her, and now every time she answered, "You didn't," she spoke with a deep sigh. Finally he came over and sat cross-legged in front of her, put his hands on her shoulders, and, gripping her with steadily increasing force and peering into her face, his eyes flickering like two flames, whispered hoarsely, "I killed her!" She leaned exhausted against his chest and said, "Yes, you killed her."

Once only he said, "Will you die with me?" She withdrew her face from his chest, and for some reason looked slowly around the room as though to brand the image of it on her retina. Then lightly she replied, "All right," and buried her face in his chest again. She felt no emotion other than a melancholy at the thought that the room would still be there after she'd gone. "Ah, but you have to live longer than your mother did, don't you," he murmured in a sort of agreement, and after a while he continued to himself: "This girl has to stay alive till she can feel that she's older than her mother; she has to become more of a woman than her mother."

Every night, after such scenes, he would tenderly put her to bed. She sank quickly into sleep while he lay stroking her hair. But as she slept she nevertheless had the constant sensation of her face, her breasts, her whole body being gazed at, and sometimes her skin would creep with a sudden chill. Finally, the sensation disappeared, and then she was somehow aware that the man beside her had grown quiet, and only the shadow of him crossed her sleep. Yet not entirely, for again and again she saw a shape like that of an old man sitting shrunken at the foot of the bed, hunched over, gazing vacantly at the closed window. She saw, but her sleep remained unbroken. And then the presence vanished entirely, and she opened her eyes to see his pale figure leaving the room.

The same thing would be repeated time and time again until dawn broke. Finally she managed to grasp the situation. Still half asleep, she slipped on her robe, neither surprised nor flustered. She caught up with him just a little way beyond the apartment and settled down to follow behind without a word until he should give in. In the beginning he walked along purposefully enough, but compared to that first evening he seemed to have little perseverance, and after turning the third corner he came to a complete halt. "Let's go back," she said, coming up beside him and taking his arm as he stood there, his head tilted in bewilderment, and set about leading him home. "What are you looking for?" she asked, and he replied, "I'm looking for the apartment." When she asked whose apartment, a look of uneasiness came over his face, but he didn't put up any resistance. However, once they had settled back into bed and she had begun to doze off, he was immediately up and off once more. Again and again this happened, and with each time he walked less far, until finally, near dawn, she put her head out the door and there he was, standing bewildered on the street just in front of her building. But the pace of his comings and goings had also increased, so that in the end she had no time even to lie down, but simply sat on the bed watching his restless movements, her sight dim with exhaustion.

After a night of this sort of thing, he would go to sleep with apparent relief once dawn broke. Sometimes he would get her to open the window, and he would stare out at the lightening sky and say "Ah, I feel as though I've just woken up from some dream. I've been an awful trouble to you, haven't I."

Once he murmured tearfully, "'When I wake quiet in the dawn. . . .'" And although up until that point she had been thinking, "It just can't go on this way, the defeat is hard to accept but I really should get in touch with his wife and have her take him to the hospital," now, hearing him talk like this, she felt instead that she would never hand him over till he was well again, and then she'd send him back and make out that nothing had happened. And she would wait for his breathing to grow regular with sleep, tenderly wiping his face and chest with a damp towel, then lie down beside him and sink straight into sleep, only to be pushed out of bed almost immediately by his outflung limbs. Now and again he groaned deep from some nightmare, but she didn't even have the strength to lift her head from where she lay beside the bed. And what would the people next door be thinking, hearing that animal voice crying out, from midday onward?

His nightly telephone calls were made from her room. In the middle of the battle over whether he had killed his sister, he would lift the receiver, turn on the radio and turn up the volume of the music, and proceed to blurt out to the person on the other end his confessions of being a murderer.

She listened fearfully, but at this stage she herself felt so confused that she couldn't make out whether the other person interpreted all this as madness or not. Sometimes he would dial someone again later in the night and murmur quietly and earnestly, and she would half-open her eyes from the bed, thinking that perhaps he had calmed down at last; but when he put the receiver down his face grew hard again, and his comings and goings continued till daybreak.

From the fourth day she stopped going out to shop, not wanting people to see her shockingly thin face, so the evening meal became a dreary business of rice and whatever else was available. His appetite had finally begun to fade, and except for mealtimes and the period between midnight and dawn, he lay dozing on the bed. All perseverance had gone from his nightly hunts, too, and he ceased to go beyond earshot of the room, so as dawn approached she no longer got up from the bed but simply lay there listening for his footsteps to halt and then return.

On the sixth day their meals consisted only of rice and salt. From two in the morning he lay exhausted face down on the bed and didn't move. "We may lie sleeping like this till we're both dead," she thought as she descended into the forgotten sweetness of night sleep. After a long while, footsteps set off from in front of the apartment, went straight on into the distance, and disappeared. Was that some passerby? she wondered, and feeling about beside her with eyes still shut she found the bed was empty.

She didn't panic. She pulled her robe on over her night-gown, carefully combed her hair, slipped into her sandals and went out. She had no idea where she was going, in fact, but she was sustained by the conviction that she would soon find him. Her feet bore her along purposefully of their own accord, following the road he had walked that first evening, and at each corner they seemed unfalteringly to know which way to turn. Not that the roads led on to some totally unfamiliar landscape—they all ran through land none the better for having been cleared for housing, yet she instinctively chose her way among the roads by whether they had or lacked a certain look. She felt, too, that somehow her senses were relying on whether the scent of water, of grass, was strong or only faint in the air. Thus, led by an instinct rather like that of a sleepwalker, she proceeded on after him from crossroad to crossroad, becoming neither weary nor discouraged, until after a long time she came upon a vast stretch of grassy vacant land and halted in confusion. It was a place she was sure she'd passed about half an hour ago, a place not so very far from her own apartment.

And now her sixth sense suddenly failed her. The road became expressionless. She set off walking again, finding herself for some reason bewailing the fact that this wasn't how a road should be. Even if you come upon a road for the first time in your life, she thought, surely it at least has a certain look to it, a faint resonance of some distant memory. As things stood, there seemed no way to proceed. And after ten minutes, she found herself passing the same patch of vacant land again. She tried to walk on in the belief that this time it was a different road, but it only led her to the same place yet again, and quicker than the last time.

And before she knew it, she found herself drawn into a sort of endless circling. A dreamlike sensation took hold of her. On she walked, and then at some point just as she was turning a corner she caught sight of him a hundred and fifty feet ahead, cutting across an intersection to disappear again. She didn't quicken her pace, however—it was as though the pace she must walk at had somehow been decided for her. She had no doubt now that, somewhere close by, he was walking in circles just as she was. At every corner there was a sense of his having passed a moment before her. Each was drawing the other, yet by the merest fraction they always failed to meet. Then suddenly, the sense of him walking nearby faded. It wasn't replaced by a total emptiness, however; rather, it seemed that he was now sitting down somewhere. In another moment she was back at the vacant land lying between the modern residences. The sky was slowly beginning to pale. "I'll wait till it gets a bit lighter," she thought, and she squatted down at the foot of a telephone pole.

At that instant she felt, in her own body, her dead mother. She had no memory of ever having seen her squatting thus by the roadside in the dawn—her mother had died when she was only six, so even her face she could recall only dimly. But she could not recognize this heavy-thighed way of squatting as any habit of her own. She thought of how she would pass her mother's age in another two years, she thought of the times before now when she had wanted to die, and she began to sob aloud for happiness that her present self had finally begun to overlap with her mother. Even the sound of her own sobs rang in her ears with a certain distant familiarity.

When she raised her eyes, the surroundings had grown brighter. She stood up and looked at the vacant lot. It was a cramped, squalid piece of land, surrounded by a barbed wire fence, waiting there until it could fetch a good price. The summer grass grew high, but all sense of freshness had disappeared with the coming of dawn. Piles of broken concrete and red earth lay here and there. A notice said "Dumping Prohibited," but all about were heaps of old electrical equipment and rotting rubbish. She was astounded by the discovery that it was to such a place they'd been drawn, it was this that they'd been circling. Then a gust of wind miraculously made its way among the crowded buildings and blew into her face, and the grass heads bowed before it in a long wave. She began to be impressed by the place again, and was just thinking that it did after all somehow have the feeling of a wide field, when she saw his head suddenly appear above the low waves of grass. He seemed to be sitting hugging his knees, and he was gazing over at her with a startled and questioning look. How white his hair is, she thought.

"Come out!" she cried into the wind, and beckoned to him. But he just sat there, gazing steadily at her with great frightened eyes.

Suddenly she did something that surprised even herself. She pulled open the crossed front of her robe so that he could see the swell of her breasts beneath the nightgown.

He rose as though stirred by the wind and came toward her, feverishly thrusting his way through the grass and treading over the piles of rubble; and then, standing before her, straddling a break in the wire fence, the legs of his trousers soaked with dew, he gently closed her robe, murmuring, "You mustn't catch cold." He was so tender that she found herself asking dreamily, "Have I gone crazy, to end up in this place?"

"No, it's me that's mad," he replied simply. And he put his arm round her shoulders and set off walking firmly along with her, saying gently, "I've gone and caused you all this trouble. I'm not going to be crazy any more. It's all right now. So it was you who was crying, was it?" And so he led her back to the apartment, never once mistaking the road.

For a whole day he was all tenderness. Noon and evening he cooked rice gruel for her in the kitchen and carried it in to her where she lay, too dazed to be able to get up. Otherwise, they lay huddled together, dozing, while the window curtains grew light, then glimmered whitely, and then gradually darkened again. Late at night they opened their eyes, surfeited with sleep, and lay staring at the ceiling, talking vaguely of inconsequential things. The events before that morning were too oppressive to be discussed. In the night, when she slid back into sleep, he stroked her hair and seemed to be fervently murmuring something like a Buddhist hymn to himself.

When next she became aware that the room was filled with light, and quickly lifted her head, she already knew that he'd gone. As she had expected, neither coat nor shirt nor tie nor shoes were to be seen. She waited for him a whole day, and the following day she made herself distraught with the idea of his having committed suicide; but this was really only to compensate for her excessive calm. She knew, in fact, that he had gone straight back to his wife and children.

"Actually, I'm almost grateful to have been allowed to suffer with him," she told me. "Thanks to him, I've resolved to live past my mother's age. I've often had the sense of my mother in my own body since that experience. He's endured a lot for many years, and it seems only right that he should take a week or so off in the middle of his life, in the home of a woman like myself, to rest and be crazy. If it were with a different woman, the sexual aspect of it would become too intense. I don't mind if he forgets about it now it's over. I'd be happy if he simply came to see me from time to time, as though nothing had happened."

Indeed, her face wore a calm and relaxed expression as she spoke. I gazed at her in dismay. It seemed that the only

74

thing my friend had remained silent about to the end was the fact that he was in the clutches of a fatal illness. For a moment I was at a loss what to do, but I decided to say nothing. She had noticed me wince slightly, however, and was looking me straight in the eye, so, inexcusably caught off guard, I found myself telling her the truth.

"I see. He's going to die is he?" she said softly in a strangely cheerful voice, and she smiled as though amused. But her cheeks stiffened as she did so, her lips turned white and, with another attempt at a smile, she burst into tears.

"Don't you think that's a terrible way to treat me?"

The Bellwether

AMONG THE HERD OF animals peacefully spread out grazing on the grassy plain, one young one on a sudden innocent impulse raises its forelegs skyward with a little leap. The next moment it takes off in frightened flight, as if suddenly touched by some unseen breath. The gentle creatures around it pause simultaneously in their ruminating to gaze for a moment with limpid blue eyes at this childish frivolity, then seem about to return to their endless cud and settle back into languid bovine levelheadedness. But then, instead, they too suddenly begin to trot at a lazy swinging amble, almost grudgingly at first, as if some forgotten obligation to run has occurred to them. In a fine cloud of dust, the docility slowly begins to disintegrate, the animals following obliviously behind their skittish young comrade, those countless legs swishing to and fro almost like the wild swaying of a forest. Now, however, it becomes apparent that their legs as they trot onward gradually grow fraught with a new fervor. And now that fervor hesitantly crosses some fine line, and in that instant a sudden spontaneous shock wave passes through the whole herd as through a single body, from the muzzle of the leading animal to the tail tip of the animal who brings up the rear, and then alarm summons speed, and speed breeds alarm, until the tremendous brown avalanche begins to tumble, trampling the brambles underfoot, recklessly scattering a pack of savage beasts in its path, as it thunders on down toward the gently flaming horizon of the early afternoon. . . .

There was a time when this scene constantly rose before my eyes. I had just moved back to the big city after five years of living in a quiet provincial town. Needless to say, I had never been to Kenya or other such places; indeed, I had no recollection of having so much as seen a wild animal in the seven years that had passed since my student days of mountain climbing.

There was another scene too, which would rise unbidden in my mind like a personal memory. It was actually based on something I had heard long ago from a friend who in turn had read it somewhere, perhaps in some mountaineering magazine, but on recalling the story a good ten years later, I found that I had in the interval turned it arbitrarily into an image of my own. It was on some high plateau in mountainous Shinshu, that much I do remember. Ten or so horses were galloping wildly hither and thither on a summer afternoon, beneath thunderclouds hanging heavy with unreleased rain. The plateau lay spread to the sky in a long gentle slope, punctuated here and there by the strange stakelike shapes of solitary spindly birch trees—a world made for galloping. But, vast world though it was, the horses seemed unable to gallop straight for more than about six hundred feet. Whenever they approached this limit and seemed to be gathering energy for the straight rush onward, they came to a sudden halt in a body— as though they had caught sight of some fearful thing ahead—raised themselves on their hind legs to the dark clouds, white teeth bared, then turned confusedly left and right, and finally plunged away again in a different direction. I imagine the storm clouds above had heightened the electric potential in their bodies, and what distressed them was the static that their manes discharged as they quivered toward the sky. Or perhaps wherever they galloped they were startled by the flashes of lightning ahead of them. I no longer remember the details of it. But in my imagination the storm clouds calm to a dense purple mass and, in the faint light that hangs breathlessly over the earth, the horses fleeing desperately here and there in that unfenced vastness are slowly driven into an ever-tightening circle. I imagine their terror then. There on that plateau's gentle skyward slope, wherever they may run, however they may try to merge with the herd, whatever they may do, each forms with its own terror-stricken body the boundary between earth and heaven.

They say the fleetest carnivore on earth is the cheetah.

No surprise then to learn that this carnivorous beast will never fail to overtake whatever prey it chooses to pursue. Perhaps of all creatures, not excluding humans, it is the cheetah that has made for itself the most elegant and epicurean of hunting and dining lifestyles. It seems that, when a cheetah attacks a herd of grazing animals, it is not so uncouth as simply to leap on some conveniently lagging beast; no, it first makes straight for the center of the herd and then, as it runs with the animals, it makes a considered choice of the piece of game that best suits the day's appetite. When this beautiful god of death first plunges into its midst, the herd fans out a little, but otherwise it continues to gallop on as before. There are animals galloping with all their might right alongside the god of death; other animals are fleeing madly along behind it, unaware that they have long been outpaced by what they flee. And then there are those who feel the god's approach like a shiver over their skin, and their legs weaken, their haunches sink suddenly to the ground, and they gaze in awe and astonishment as he strides superbly by, not deigning to cast a glance in their direction. Yet the moment the god has passed they scramble abruptly to their feet again and, in fear and trepidation, set off following the death god once more. Once a sacrificial animal has been surrendered the stampede comes to an end; but I wonder if there is indeed any real difference for these herd animals between the fear they feel when pursued by this swift and fickle enemy, or by a more slow-footed and sedate one, or yet again by some enemy in fact nonexistent. In whichever case I would say that their frantic flight is for them a prompting of instinct, behavior dictated by their own kind of common sense, so whether the origin of the fear is known or not would have no effect on the amplitude of the fear's shock wave. It certainly seems to be the case that, once scattered calmly grazing over the field again, they have not the slightest idea if a martyr has indeed disappeared from their midst or if all their flight was only from some insubstantial terror. Perhaps it would be fair to say that for these animals there is no such thing as true panic.

Commuting to work each morning, this is the sort of ridiculous idea that I used to ponder in deep earnest in those days. "The city is a terrifying place," I would murmur to myself. Yes, and this despite the fact that I was born and bred in the city. As a student, the city meant little to me, and once I left the university and started to earn a salary, the state of my purse improved slightly and the city impinged on me even less. The only clamor that I made room for inside me was that which sat well with the clamor of the outside world, so to speak. But now, after five years of life in the provinces, coming back with wife and child to the city I'd left single, I found myself inwardly gaping in astonishment every morning at the sight of the rush-hour throngs— despite the fact that I'd traveled back and forth in packed trains since I was in my midteens.

It was the silence of those morning crowds that really

made me gape. They hadn't been so silent back in the town I'd left. There too I used to commute every morning in a packed bus, but loud voices could always be heard confabulating here and there in the crush, indeed it had the atmosphere of a kind of besuited village, and this village would descend again en masse in noisy and expressive commotion when the bus drew up in front of the stylish prefectural office building. My own life too seemed in those days to be straight out of the easygoing world of an old-style Japanese autobiographical novel. I took to doing the rounds of the drinking houses, relying on credit and without a cent on me, keeping it up till I tumbled over. Regardless of when and where I was finally turned out, it would take me no more than an hour of walking through the darkness to stumble back to my little roost. And by that stage it didn't much bother me where I slept or even whether I slept or not. I remember one snowy night a colleague and I stayed out drinking till past two, and then finally wove our way back together to our respective lodgings out beyond the very edge of the town, toying as we went with the temptation to plunge into the deep snow that lay all around us. When we reached the edge of the town and saw before us that boundless white expanse so intently absorbing the weight of the thickly falling snow, I had the overwhelming sense that it was in fact the earth that was spewing forth this fine white powder to melt upward into the soft sky. But suddenly a voice said, "Hey, you there, how long are you going to keep on walking round and round, eh?" And when I turned to look, there suddenly was the black outline of my pal, sitting in the top of a solitary low tree that stood in the middle of the field. Seeing me approach in amazement, he rose up out of the top branches, directed his pathetic chin at the far distance, and yelled, "Give me a piece of Tokyo ass!" "Not for me thanks," said I, standing at the foot of the tree and giving it a shake. At which the snow fell with a flop onto my head, and was followed by the body of my colleague, which descended quite comfortably and face upward, and buried itself with a heavy thud in the fresh snow. I lifted the body, which didn't so much as twitch, roughly hoisted it over my shoulder, and set off into the snow, surprised at what a light fellow he was for all the noise he made. It began to snow in real earnest all about me, and only the faintest sense of the town lights remained at the far bottom of the gently sloping valley. On and on it snowed, drawing an intent silence over the land. Even the sound of my footsteps was sucked immediately into that silence, leaving not the slightest reverberation. In that snow the only certain sound was the throbbing in my temples. And yet, even then I didn't feel the sort of silence around me that I felt now, in the midst of the city rush hour.

Perhaps if I had a few more brains I might have laid my disquiet to rest with a plain straightforward sociological study of the phenomenon. But when it first dawned on me that this impression of silence actually came from the queer smoothness of the crowd's flow, I was a mere cringing new-comer. Just why was it that people here didn't create any sort of commotion when they got off buses and trains, as the people back in the provinces had done? Every morning and evening they would pass through the utterly impersonal ticket gate without the least sign of irritation and flow on out evenly over the great floor, though no command to that effect had been given; on they would flow, precisely in step with the group's tempo, making no attempt to push people out of the way or force their way through anywhere, though if the density suddenly thinned somewhere they would fill the gap immediately. Then, when the crowd finally reached the stairway, the flow would slacken and mill quietly, while from up ahead it slowly tilted and began to spill downward. It was precisely like a waterfall that slides silently and smoothly over the face of a mossy rock, and induced the same vague dizziness when gazed at. . . .

The word *orderly* fits the phenomenon exactly. Can there be a more orderly movement of people anywhere in the world today? Those who make the necessary statistical calculations concerning the number of people who flow through the terminal in one minute every morning, and the size of the space that receives them, will understand that they are witnessing a daily repeated miracle. If social scientists were to prove as faithful to their science on home territory as when they apply their vaunted analytical powers to the situations of distant countries, they ought really to

undertake an analysis of this daily mass population movement. The conclusion could only be: "This is an impossibility, and therefore cannot exist." For in this case the average
person cannot be taken as statistical material. What shapes
this crowd is peculiarly disciplined humans. If, for instance,
we were to select—from among the nation's politicians, crit-
ics, editorialists, scholars, and enlightened women—those
possessing the very finest of moral opinions and pack them
together into a train (and no doubt even a thirty-carriage
train packed to absolute capacity still wouldn't hold them
all), and if we then let them loose at the terminal under
these same conditions . . . well, I really couldn't bear to
watch. Imagine the fearful tragedy likely to ensue!

But even at that stage I didn't have it in me to dare to
ask myself just *why* such orderliness. The answer was after
all a foregone conclusion: Because one has to live, because
one has to hurry. Each of us may be feeling in fact quite irri-
tated enough to begin shoving at the people around us, but
it is precisely on account of this irritation that we create as a
whole such a smooth flow. It is the regularity of the stampede, of the stampede that instinctively understands that the
more the haste, the less the speed. In this situation the worst
disturber of the peace is the person who doesn't need to hurry and so picks his own arbitrary pace. One morning, when
I'd finally managed to get off onto the terminal platform, I
quickly overtook a man of around forty, and as I did so the
sight of him from behind somehow struck me. The back

84

was held straight, the head slumped loosely forward, and that oddly serene air of his, as though stepping out into a sudden downpour without any fear of getting wet, seemed to me in some way utterly cynical. I was immediately overwhelmed with an irrational indignation. And then, in a sudden mad glee at the sheer irrationality of it, I set about roughly elbowing and shoving my way through the flow of people until I finally reached the milling throng at the ticket gate and paused for breath. There beside me suddenly stood that same man. The outline of his face was strangely, sinisterly regular, and that face was gazing quietly at the floor as though somehow apologetic at finding himself standing there beside me. The sight stirred me to an even greater rage. When I had streamed with everyone out through the ticket gate my anger gave an added keenness to my reflexes, and I moved swiftly forward through the gaps that ceaselessly appear and disappear in the flow, endlessly overtaking hurrying people, until in no time I had cut across the great floor and come up behind the slow pour of people descending the stairs. Then I noticed, about two yards to my left, a man just taking the first step down, searching hurriedly in his breast pocket as he did so, and there was no question, it was the same man, moving smoothly along just as though he'd arrived there ahead of me. An uncanny sensation crept over me. Then suddenly I became transformed into a one-man rebellion in the midst of the crowd. I forced my way down the stairs, thrusting people aside left and right with my shoulders, till I reached the underpass and crossed it almost at a run. When my subway train finally moved off and I glimpsed that man, his decent decorous face raised and facing straight ahead, slide away among the people left behind on the platform, oh then what frantic joy I gave myself up to, though I was leaning at such an angle in the carriage that it was difficult to stay upright. But when I got out into the morning light I suddenly thought to stop and buy some cigarettes in front of the station, and as I calmly set off again with one stuck in my mouth a shape slid quickly past me and went walking away serenely into the downpour without so much as hunching its shoulders against it. Then it was that I began to fear I had come back to the city only to turn neurotic.

I certainly had sufficient reason to be neurotic. Coming back to the city, everyone around me seemed quite unnervingly competent. And in fact they were. At the office, I once watched—with all the chilling sensations of staring at a naked sword—a man five years my senior sitting quietly at a corner desk and completing in one day work the equivalent of which, when I was in the provinces, had taken me and two colleagues three days to complete, and that with a great deal of fuss and a round of celebratory drinks on the evening it was finally done. Obviously, here I could only face up to my own incompetence. In fact, I grew so pious that I even decided to beg the man for guidance when an opportunity presented itself. However, one evening when I was leaving work with my new colleagues the man passed us from behind, and as he did so he meekly lowered his head and smiled a sort of smudgy smile. When his form grew sufficiently distant, one of my colleagues informed me, "That guy's an inveterate family man. Just the other day, when we were up to our eyeballs in work, he went off at five saying it was his kid's birthday. It meant we were there till past ten that night." There was something about the look of this man not unreminiscent of the retreating figure of that other man in the downpour.

There was a certain rather outrageous fantasy that I used to indulge in in those days, in the midst of the morning throngs. It revolved around the question of whether it would be possible then and there to arouse panic in that quiet crowd. It's not from any real external cause that panic arises; it can only result from some essentially internal phenomenon. If, for instance, someone who had every appearance of a decent law-abiding citizen were suddenly to swing around with a convincing look of alarm and set off at a run, elbowing his way desperately against the flow, and if this alarm were to cross at a single leap some emotional boundary in the surrounding people and enter that state of almost physical resonance where the chest tingles and vibrates, then maybe ten people would unconsciously be dragged in and, before they knew it, run perhaps ten paces. And if ten people began to run, among them there would undoubtedly be one docile "sensible" one, the sort whose stoutness of belly produces a strong impression of weighty experience in the business of living. This is the point where it all suddenly teeters on the edge of a steep downward slope. And the reason is, that we search out the docile sensible types even among passing strangers and use such people as background characters, as it were, in our endless unconscious monitoring of the equilibrium of our own perceptions of reality. By way of proof, isn't it true that whenever we get thoroughly sick of our own perceptions of reality, the "sensible" people around us suddenly seem to have disappeared, and all that meets the eye are fanatic middle-aged faces?

So I would try and imagine, right then and there, one of these sensible types suddenly breaking into a frightened run. After all, it's not necessarily true that primitive fear appears any less overtly in this kind of person. So the sensible person shows the whites of his eyes and begins to run. Despite how ludicrous such a sight would be—or indeed, precisely because of it—the panic would probably start to overflow. Even people who hadn't witnessed the first moment of alarm would begin to run, and those who had taken flight in the beginning would now be running with no idea of what it was that pursued them. And so the mob would be off. Even if it were all to calm down again after only ten seconds, and turn out to be no more than what people frowningly dismiss as a momentary and inexplicable confusion, that really wouldn't alter matters. After all, ten seconds is a long time. Everyone who had run ten steps then, those who had run perhaps five uncertain steps, even those who had done no more than widen their eyes in momentary terror, would know that they had shied at a shadow, and the humiliation of it would grow into a deep unease, which in turn gives way to an increasing sense of dismay, until within each person the panic would be thundering down toward the dark horizon, trampling the brambles underfoot. . . .

Such was the nonsense I used to think. Perhaps it was the excessive orderliness in the flow of the crowds that drove me to this sort of fantasy. At all events, it was the product of that slight loss of reality experienced by one just returned to the big city. Outside me the city rose, clamorous and taciturn, and as yet inside me I had neither the uproar nor the silence to contend with it. A true child of nature would soon lose his internal balance in this situation and simply go to pieces or else would strike out into the outside world, one of the two; but in my case I was at bottom a city man, and with dependents to support besides, so it was natural enough that I should submit to this vast reality. But when on the outside you submit to reality docilely and behave "sensibly" while privately you're still something of an outsider, a strange stillness arises within you, and through it all manner of weird ideas pass in various forms. And so I sank back into the fantasy once again, this time to ponder the useless question of what sort of character would be a likely one for the man who first begins to run at the outset of the panic. And no sooner said than a particular kind of look, a particular kind

of expression, presented itself to my mind. This was alto-
gether too much for me. I'm somewhat fastidious in that I
don't care for mental overindulgence in things that have no
basis in reality. I felt my own thoughts beginning to move
out of control. And then, the unfamiliar word *bellwether*
came along to save me. "That's what a bellwether is," I said
to myself, "the animal who takes the lead." And with the
neat resonance of that strange term, I determined to round
off this particular train of thought, which had begun to turn
distinctly odd.

But once a word has been conjured up, like a bad drunk
or an inquisitive woman, you can't shake it loose. I thought
I'd tied things off nicely with that knowing "That's what a
bellwether is," but after a while I became aware of an odd
thing. The word *bellwether* was taught to me by a young linguist with whom I occasionally went drinking in the
provinces and, according to his explanation of it, a bellwether is the most outstandingly powerful beast in the herd,
the boss animal who's been through the mill, the one who
unerringly heads the flock in flight from the enemy's fangs.
In the case of livestock, the drover has only to set this one
beast moving and the whole herd is in the palm of his hand.
Granted though, from time to time this animal will suddenly start to gallop for no reason, and then it will plunge the
entire herd into a meaningless stampede. It may have been
because that linguist told me all this that I recalled the word
bellwether at this point in my thoughts.

And yet, the funny thing is, when I muttered, "That's what a bellwether is," the image that was in my mind was a far cry from that of a "sensible," been-through-the-mill sort of creature. . . . Among the docile beasts spread out quietly grazing over the grassy plain, a young one bored with playing suddenly raises his head on impulse and gives an odd leap. Whereupon the herd is shaken by a real fear, and the next instant it is on the run. . . . The word *bellwether* brought to mind a creature with the eyes of an infant, ingenuously coy yet somewhere also fanatic.

On the other hand, the image of that correct yet somehow cynical man in the downpour also stuck firmly in my mind. With every lull in the crowd's flow, that serene gait had fallen in alongside my own irate one quite uncannily. Could that be the tempo that controls the herd? And was it perhaps his very grasp of the fact that however quickly or slowly you walk, it comes to the same thing, which lent to the correct figure a somehow cynical air? For the idea that it makes no difference either way is a truly cynical one. In this way does the cynic do away with the various pangs of conscience he may feel, leaving himself free to refine his own pleasures. According to my conception of it, the cynic provides himself with just such a subtle and flexible philosophy as will serve to protect his psychological pleasures from being sullied. Only a dog lashes out at someone else from the pain of his own guilty conscience. These days, the insolent cynic who has sex with some woman in public, then turns and yells at the shocked and gaping bystanders, "We have nothing to hide!" has actually come into his own. When you come to think of it, I suppose I should have felt a real empathy with that man in the downpour. But the fact is that the moment I laid eyes on him I was seized with indignant rage. There he was, shoulders thrown back un-self-consciously, his back held straight, and above it, abruptly, the head ever so meekly lowered, stepping coolly and delicately among the throng as though he were stepping from rock to rock to avoid treading the moss in some elegant Japanese garden—such a figure, in fact, as would give offense to no one, yet to my eyes it appeared a figure of quite unscrupulous dissipation.

On the whole, I don't care for the kind of man who sinks into his own private world without thought for the eyes of those around him. In the case of those few people who have become deeply involved with my private self, I have felt this as almost a shameful part of me and myself as equivalently a part of their personal shame, and that we have no choice but simply to continue to maintain this connection quietly and privately until death. But aside from these cases, I held stubbornly to the belief, especially at that stage in my life, that people's behavior should be cut-and-dried. Blatantly giving oneself over to one's private self in the midst of other people is like a child suddenly rushing in with a cry of "Hurrah!" to a room where people are nervously handling high explosives. But was that man in the downpour after all vulnerable to criticism in this regard? Wasn't he firmly enveloped in the appropriate attire of the docile city folk, even down to the conscientious briefcase in hand? Furthermore, had he really any option but to walk in that manner, having once understood that however high-handedly one may thrust ahead, when it comes down to it one can never get out of step with the crowd? And yet for all that, whenever I recalled the sight of him, I was immediately roused to an indignant rage.

It was just the same with that superior of mine. For a long time I was simply too stupid to notice, but in fact those around him seemed to consider him something of a joke, the way they would a monk or a scholar. "But he's a competent person, surely?" I asked one of my colleagues.

"Oh yes, he's competent enough all right," he assured me. "But he never initiates anything himself—seems to avoid it almost out of some odd principle. He's so fastidious it makes you sick."

And then I began to observe this man more closely. Sure enough there was something ludicrous about, for instance, the way he would quietly, radiantly persevere with his one particular way of eating noodles. But when I looked at that correct face, at the eyes always moist like those of a child, the unnervingly defenseless lips, I began to think that this man was probably the kind who, once he really set in on something, wouldn't be able to hold himself within the framework of the particular task at hand. In this case, there was no denying he was right in the way he lived. It is only

humanly decent to live this way, pallid and benign, if it's in
order to avoid afflicting the people around you with your
fanatic behavior. Nevertheless, I clung to my belief that it
was somehow obscene to go guarding oneself like this. Surely this "sensible" prudence was actually preserving him in a
state of endless infantile fanaticism. . . .

And so my image of the bellwether remained insubstantial. Yet just because it is insubstantial doesn't mean that an
image doesn't affect you. Even if you can't call the overall
appearance to mind, there can be a certain suggestion of the
features; and even if no feature of the face occurs to you, you
might still sense a certain look directed at you. I began to
hate that bellwether in good and earnest.

I may not have been able to gain a clear picture of what
sort of creature the bellwether was, but I certainly had a
clear idea of what he wasn't. He was not the intensely individual type. An intensely individual person can drag the surrounding people along with him for quite a distance, be it
only through their sense of discomfort and humiliation.
There have actually been such cases. But sheer force of per-
sonality can simply exert no effect on these smooth-flowing
big-city masses. Indeed, the very fact of being inside that
flow would surely preclude the very possibility of intense
individuality. On the other hand, even such a huge flow is
far from invulnerable. There is after all a great emptiness
within people when they are intent on nothing further than
the instant of their next step, just as with people absorbed in

manipulating a complex machine. And when that emptiness is suddenly jolted, as when we're knocked awake from a deep sleep, it is easy to respond with extremely swift and primitive reactions. What is more, if such a reaction does occur it occurs simultaneously throughout the whole crowd, where everyone is walking at the same tempo led by the same necessity. And once there is confusion, that over-rational orderliness crumbles at a single stroke. Yet no, if it were simply a matter of a stampede's order being shattered, there would still be hope, for it would be quite possible for us to awaken at some point from that mass existence and return to our individual selves. More frightening is the possibility that we might dissociate ourselves from the scream that spontaneously rises up within us, and instead take off at a thunderous run, preserving chill and intact the discipline of the stampede. Once this happens a few people may indeed be trampled underfoot, but this too is merely part of the stampede's internal order. It is said that from time to time that which is overly rational will suddenly swing full circle into irrationality, but it's not actually so dramatic a thing as that, surely. In fact it's more that the overly rational will on a certain day, and without the slightest alteration, suddenly be irrational. Just like a wild animal crossing a bright field and, without altering pace, suddenly entering the dark shadow of the trees beyond.

Nevertheless, I thought to myself, supposing for a moment that there might be a person capable of inducing madness in this smooth orderliness, even if only briefly, what sort of man would he be? He might well be the sort of person who neither makes others uncomfortable nor inspires any strong feelings one way or the other about him—such a harmless-seeming person that no one could have any way to resist him. With a smile utterly depersonalized and insipid, such a person could pass smoothly through people's emptiness to enter unabashed a part of them that a cruder individuality could as a matter of course never reach, and once there . . . push the button. At this point in my train of thought, I was assailed by a sudden vivid image of the infantile purity, the animal-like shamelessness of those eyes, and I ground my teeth. Yet those were eyes that knew everything, and within them there was a vague sycophancy, a sense that they were soliciting one's tacit understanding.

If this hatred once took hold of me in the midst of the morning throngs, I would then be forced to spend virtually the entire day feeling thoroughly disagreeable to myself. On such days as these, the most I could manage with any sense of pleasure was a mute machinelike performance of my duty. All enterprises above that basic level, those that involved any kind of self-expression, induced a sense of loathing. When reading a newspaper or magazine, like some jealous dog I would sniff out a futile malice behind most of the opinions expressed there. I would constantly find myself caught short by the discovery that what seemed a thoroughly reasonable passing opinion was in fact saying quite the opposite of what its moral language suggested, indeed seemed to be rejecting everything completely, even throwing overboard the argument that the author had been so carefully developing, so that in effect he was temporarily abandoning himself to some deep-seated venom, like a drunkard falling flat on his face and suddenly yelling abuse on the main street. There were opinions that I could see were actually scratching away madly at the itch of their own malice, like some mangy dog, under cover of making a quite plausible criticism of others. Whatever the opinion, it was always a mild and reasonable one, but there were always somehow two or three words too many, and in these unnecessary words the underlying malice was simply crying out. Or again, when a pedestrian steps awkwardly out to cross the road in front of a car that has slowed a little as it approached the crossing, think of that look, charged with faint animosity, which passes between pedestrian and driver. It's not that either of them lack the imaginative power to put themselves in the other's place, but just that at that moment the driver is a Driver, and the pedestrian, a Pedestrian; hence the futile malice between them. That sort of thing used to exhaust me, and it made me hate myself then for being so sensitive to hatred. I would do my best to relax my shoulders, straighten my back, and walk through the crowd at a leisurely pace, repeating to myself like a spell the meaningless words "When you get out of bed on the wrong side, nothing goes right all day." Then I would sense suddenly within myself that figure walking coolly off into the fierce downpour without so much as a flinch of the shoulders. And then suddenly an infantile figure would be pushing his way past me through the crowd, with the fanatic look of one perhaps out for further entertainment for the evening.

EVERY MORNING SOME SUCH idle newcomer's fantasy would grip me; and then one morning it happened that a simple three-minute delay in the subway trains created in my particular subway station a crush huge enough to fill a major festival event. I managed somehow to slip through under the yellow rope that was closing off the station and forcing the flow of people into two streams, and went down to the subway and attached myself to the tail end of the vast eddy at the ticket gate. The flow was quite hopelessly banked up, but that still didn't prevent people from shuffling their feet forward little by little; they seemed to be straining every nerve in the search for any space in which to move the tiniest bit farther. However, a little later a loudspeaker announced a further delay of two or three minutes. Then, predictably, the tiny movements came to a sudden halt. People began to shiver slightly, as though they'd woken abruptly out of some uneasy dream of a wild gallop, and out from beneath the suddenly relaxed tension there appeared the unadorned and somehow shameless faces of the newly woken. Even the young girls had this look. I watched, unnerved, as that clever clothing of theirs, not without its allurements while everyone was in motion, now suddenly seemed to lose its charm and instead to cling dully round their bodies, as each girl stood there almost leaning her forehead into the broad back of the man ahead. Those faces had about them a bleak transparency too depraved to be revealed even to their closest intimates. Then there were the artless faces of other girls who made the kind of gesture from which one hastily averts one's eyes, such as putting a hand round behind them to touch the suddenly lascivious swelling beneath their skirt. Newcomer that I was, I could only stare about me wide-eyed, thinking inanely, "Solitude leads to shamelessness."

Before long I spied two middle-aged men over beside a pillar where the crowd was relatively thin, standing deep in conversation facing the pillar with their shoulders together, excluding the eyes of the surrounding people. They looked exactly like old-fashioned merchants silently and animated-ly gesturing prices at each other, but judging from the back they appeared too mild-mannered for merchants. Sheer boredom induced my imagination to run away on me, tempted by what an interesting scene it would create to put this tall, pale, and correct pair alongside the downpour man and that superior of mine. Then I became a little more serious, and I thought to myself that it must be very pressing business that couldn't keep till they could get somewhere out of earshot. And yet, how tremulous they both seemed.

As they talked together in such deep earnest, nodding heavily to each other, they kept glancing about them as though fearful of something. Every few moments they would turn and gaze blankly in different directions, ascertaining together with stealthy eye movements that no one's attention had been drawn to them, then back they would plunge into their private discussion. Occasionally one of them would begin to lose awareness of the surrounding eyes in his absorption, whereupon the other would poke him firmly in the belly with the tips of his fingers as though reproving him for his rashness while craning his neck ingenuously, doubly watchful to make up for his pal's obliviousness. What on earth could this matter of such moment be, that bound them so agitatedly together, and in such a place? Surely such caution was unnecessary. The people around were for the moment far too alone with themselves to be bothered listening in on someone else's conversation. Even if it did happen to fall on their ears, they wouldn't have had the wherewithal to pin it down and connect it with their own preoccupations, so it could only have gone in one ear and out the other for them. The two were more alone there than they would have been in the middle of a completely deserted plain. Mightn't they perhaps be planning in fact to blow up the subway then and there? . . .

But I was grossly mistaken. I finally understood this once the flow of people had moved a little and my angle of vision was slightly altered. In fact it was no discussion, it was actually a minor shoving match they were engaged in, breath bated; to wit, an argument, two stags locking horns in passing.

Yet there was certainly no mistake in what I'd observed. While these two were engaged in their confrontation, they were nevertheless doing their best to protect each other from prying eyes, one peering round to the left, the other keeping an eye out on the right. There was an intimate, cringing sense of solidarity there; if some third person were to innocently approach they would both close up tight together against him. These two would be the sort of family man to have a couple of kids at home, but looking closely, I could see the infantile trembling of their shoulders. They stood there ridiculously—shielded by one another's backs, arms clamped firmly to their sides, locked together in combat from the wrists down—surreptitiously battling it out exactly in the manner of a man and woman sneaking a forbidden tryst together. I became aware, watching those calm faces making their measured survey of the surroundings, of a vivid pathos there, the pathos of those who are slipping irrevocably down into the depths of an emotion.

There was something truly uncanny in it. Dark emotion had already well and truly crossed the brink and come pouring out, and yet prudence was still at work, exactly like a machine left running alone in a room. Yet again I found myself recalling the downpour man and that superior of mine, and I scowled ferociously. Then suddenly on my own face I sensed the scowling features of a lunatic. This crazy fantasy of mine certainly seemed to be having dire effects. . . .

But a little later, when the crush had finally begun to flow again and I looked back on the episode of a few moments before, I began to see it in an odd new light. Perhaps it wasn't only for their own sakes that those two were afraid of people's eyes discovering their mad behavior, it was also for the sake of those around them. It almost seemed, in fact, that what they were doing was essentially the same job as that performed by those who try to shield from sight a wounded person with his terrible blood. In which case theirs would no longer have been that individual form of insecurity known as timidity. Quite possibly, what loomed over their every action was the fear of that stampede hidden in the midst of the smooth movements and quiet lulls in the surrounding mass. After all, a man who lives beneath a dome that might at any moment collapse on his head would unconsciously keep his voice lowered even during the most abandoned fit of bellowing.

It was undoubtedly as a result of the peculiar way a newcomer's mind works that at that point I suddenly found myself thinking of weapons of mass extermination.

Unlike some, I never have been one for using the occasional meditation on mass extermination weapons to whip up my pallid sense of morality and to liquidate all the other diverse pangs of conscience at the same time. I know that whipping is basically the same sordid act whether the victim is oneself or someone else. But there was no avoiding the fact that, faced with the thought of such weapons, my imagination sickened and paled. I certainly had no trouble imagining the weapon sitting there in some underground room, giving off a faint metallic gleam, with someone aiming it straight over us. I could also picture to myself the possibility that the person who picked up the receiver for that call to press the button would already have laid a detailed plan for moves toward conciliation, and that the tacit understanding of the enemy would be a part of the plan's premise. And that wasn't all. It was not even beyond the powers of my imagination to conceive that it might be, for example, some delightful young man's sense of poignant remorse that presses the button on us—given that even such a weapon is after all only a machine, and it's only really a matter of pressing its button, and there's essentially no necessity to wait for the appropriate signal from someone. All this I could somehow contemplate. But my imagination simply couldn't meet the final reality. Time and again I would imagine my spirit hanging about outside the control room, muttering to itself that it was hopeless, that it couldn't get itself into that room and actually see that bright red button no matter how courageously the imagination was steeled. But all such exercises were futile. This reality was hidden behind no seemly veil; it was an all-too-blatant one. Faced with it, I could summon up no picture, and the humiliation of this was what made my imaginative powers sicken and fade. And indeed, this is how things stood also where the idea of panic was concerned.

But then again, I thought, people have no option but to live to the full, even though it be under the threat of such weapons. Even beneath a crumbling dome people can manage to live fairly fanatically, caught up in their love and hatred of those things around them. We humans have always, whatever passing timidity and prudence may momentarily grip us, ultimately possessed what could be called a giant's eye; even faced with a completely senseless and terrifying explosion, this eye has always been capable of observing all tragedy with a kind of gentle oceanic ruthlessness, and affirming that essential humanness that will nevertheless continue to survive it. But when this giant's eye gazes upon the truly annihilatory power that humans have finally made their own, it can no longer continue to affirm the unrestrained activity of that human essence, and here it disintegrates like a Sphinx whose riddle has at last been solved. Then, among the ruins, human reason lays the whip to its emaciated self, and sets itself up as ludicrous dictator, witnessing with suspicion and dread how irrationality prevails the more around it the harsher human reason itself becomes. And yet, in the end I could not but acknowledge this dictator. . . .

WHEN MY FANTASY REACHED THIS point, it became simply disgusted by its own stupidity, and fell silent. Finally, it seemed, the city had pervaded my inner self. Every morning with scarcely any variation I would stand there being carried along in the train, peering at my neighbor's morning paper, then move on out through the terminal to be crammed inside another subway train, absently pondering the bits and pieces of the article that had lodged themselves in my brain, and I never for a moment considered that the intense quietness of this crowd of which I myself was a part had any relation to those fears of annihilation. Just around that time I became involved in some very difficult work. It was the kind of work that made exhausting demands, not on the whole of me but on two or three special areas of myself. In order to somehow get this work done, there was nothing for it but to become the same sort of ferociously competent person as those around me. Sick at heart at the prospect, I started in on the task. The reason for my depression was that I knew full well that, if the work didn't get done, there would be hell to pay, and that if it did get done, it would be accepted without comment. Even if I kicked up a fuss, I would end up doing the work anyway. It was still too early, I felt, for me to become a competent person. Those first three months made my nerves jangle day and night. Things continued to go far from smoothly even after that, but finally there came a time when I began to feel the sort of sensation one feels when contentedly listening to the sound of a train as it glides out of the station and sets off on its journey. My perceptions had become sharpened to a fine cold edge, whereas my emotions had sunk into a state of torpor. And sometimes, while submerged in my work, I would suddenly find I was murmuring to myself, with a sensation like sighing and turning over in sleep, "How pleasant it would be not to have to bother with the trouble of being human any more, to simply turn myself over completely to this smooth machine-like operation and be done with it." I had become a little too humanized in the five years of living in that quiet backwater. Now I was just getting back to normal again, that was all. That's what I thought to myself; and soon a year had passed.

But there seems to be a kind of slow-moving yearly tide within the human heart. Those senseless morning fantasies of mine were a little like water in the hollow of a rock, which very faintly rises and falls with the far sea's tidal ebb and flow. Bewitched by the smooth run of work, I had first wanted to become a machine, then had finally forgotten even this desire; and then suddenly, after a year had passed, those unregenerate fantasies came flooding out again.

But now I was no longer a newcomer.

ONE MORNING, AS EVER, WE came streaming out onto the broad station floor from the pileup around the ticket gate, and as I searched about for some means of quickening my pace I noticed that there was a tiny space around the righthand pillar of the line of three pillars ahead of me, and I betook myself there, like a particle sucked into a vacu-um. Then I saw that there was a man crouching at the foot of the pillar, and I hastened to move on past him.

More than likely the nastiness of a hangover had caught up with him in the packed train's stuffy atmosphere. He'd managed to hold it back as far as this, but finally apparently he simply couldn't go another step. My own body was not without its memories in this regard. Assuming he'd come in on the most recent express train, it would have been fifteen minutes since he'd left the last stop, and it would also have taken quite a while to get through the press at the ticket gate, which was even fiercer than usual, and make his way this far. With a bad hangover, this is no small ordeal. Little shivers were running through that courageous body, which crouched there hunched over apologetically, and I could see from his back the signs of the slow mounting of the urge to vomit. His hands were desperately clutching at the marble pillar, but they could get no grip on the smooth surface, and the effect of this sight was, poignantly, both sad and funny. But suddenly I found myself wondering how we around him appeared to those eyes of his as they clouded over with the anguish of the slow upsurge of nausea. Quite possibly, our feet might seem to him like a great forest thundering over the ground. . . .

"This is panic," I muttered to myself, but I didn't under-stand what it was I'd said.

Just what was it I was witnessing? A man crouching quietly at the foot of a pillar, unintentionally creating a slight obstruction to the traffic around him. And something gently surging up within him, softly shaking his body. Then, as the nausea reaches its peak, it suddenly changes instead into a strange sensation neither pleasant nor unpleasant, a deep calm spreads through him, and finally from the far depths of that calm, slowly, like a great gentle fish, a feeling of suffocation comes rising up. Then the pit of his stomach suddenly tightens, all awareness of his surroundings disintegrates completely, and softly like snow the vomit begins to pour forth. And all around this utterly stark solitude, creatures go thundering by, shaking the earth.

I perceived a faint distaste and sympathy flicker over the faces of people as they passed, making a tiny detour around the pillar. They had seen the pitiful sight of a man helplessly absorbed in his own suffering in the midst of a crowd. He embodied what at this particular moment they most wish to avoid for themselves. But in the same moment this presence becomes the quiet focal point of the surrounding crowd, and the awareness of those people hurrying on by is sucked as if by vacuum back to where he crouches. Suddenly they picture themselves hunched at the foot of that pillar, deep in an all-too-obvious, all-too-innocent, and helpless self-engrossment. And they feel obscurely the thundering rush of the terrifying stampede all around them. Fearfully they watch from within themselves the stampede of the mass of which they themselves are a part. . . .

All this I took in at a single glance, and I said to myself, "This must be the bellwether."

ONE NIGHT ABOUT TWO months later, a group of demonstrators became involved in a short scuffle with the riot police when they attempted to move from the park out onto the main street, and in the wake of their having inevitably been forced back inside the park, there I suddenly was, left lying unconscious on the street, being guarded by the police. It wasn't only the result of my own particular stupidity that I ended up like this; the students had suddenly come flooding out from an unexpected quarter, and ten or so people who happened to be passing got caught up in the fray. But I'd just got that work done and out of the way at last, and admittedly I was in a rather dazed condition. Furthermore, I must actually have been fairly drunk from early evening onward to have been wandering around for no reason in such a place. At all events, I was the only one of all the students and passersby to end up sprawled on the street.

The police apparently had a suspicion at first that I might actually be one of the agitators. It seems there had been a large besuited man among the students, who would suddenly show himself in the midst of the youngsters, waving a placard above his head like a windmill and crying "Cross! Cross!" and in general urging the students on whenever they began to waver in their determination to cross the street. A young riot squad policeman apparently suggested that I somehow resembled him. Thank heavens, the police soon realized that I wasn't a large man. Nevertheless, they seem to have checked on my identity the following day, probably wanting a lead on the circumstances that lay behind the whole affair. They wouldn't have found any hint of what they were after there, of course. My colleagues knew of the suspicion that rested on me, probably because the police had gone to my office, and they showed up at the hospital, a row of gleeful faces unanimously singing the praises of my valor. Even the section head came along and cracked a lot of jokes about Marxism and Leninism, then left again. What he meant by this was that I needn't worry about what the company might think of the affair. As for me, I simply considered that I'd met with an accident. Yet from time to time I would recall what that young riot squad policeman had said. I'm not a large man, of course. Furthermore, there's no way I can be said to look any different from the average bourgeois university graduate, and being knocked cold wouldn't have made any difference in that. And yet, it was precisely this appearance of mine that the policeman thought he identified in that agitator; otherwise, why (despite the fact that it's perfectly obvious I'm not a large man) would he tell the authorities that I resembled this fellow?

I can remember being badly knocked around by the students. The sight of someone being flung about unresistingly could conceivably appear in fact more like someone arrogantly flailing about and laying down the law, I suppose. And no doubt too it would be a fine piece of entertainment to shove a placard into the hands of a decent burgher who's staggering around in a state of bewilderment. . . . At any rate, I ended by being punched in the pit of the stomach and losing consciousness. I think this was also the doing of one of the students. Well, if I were a student and witnessed a decent citizen carelessly allowing himself to be sucked into that whirlpool, performing a sort of idiot wavering skeleton dance in the midst of it, I would probably have done the same. I don't call that unreasonable. Though my skin was certainly prickling with fear of The Crowd, I felt no anger toward the students themselves. In fact, every time I glimpsed those thoroughly decent, thoroughly common-place-looking faces, faces quite capable of achieving a simple happiness, lit up by the flashing lights of the police cars, extreme sadness overwhelmed me. "No my friends, there's no winning this one," said a voice within me. "Don't you see that sort of violence is precisely in line with the ways of this world?" Yes, I was certainly pretty drunk. One should never make the mistake of believing that people turn fanatic when drunk. In fact, the drunker you are, the more the mind grows chill and calm. It's the surroundings that become more fanatic.

But I suspect that riot squad man still can't quite rid himself of his impression even now. He would be judging from the number of experiences one so young would have

had, and this sort of delusion would be the result. Still, I
suppose there's nothing to prevent someone claiming that it
was actually in no way a delusion, and that in fact I was that
large man. When this thought occurred to me as I lay quietly in bed there alone, I somehow sensed this "I" moving out
through the grubby glass of the hospital window and over
the roofs of the houses, to spread out above the main street,
mingling with the voice of the loudspeaker, which came
floating up from the distant business district. If that accident produced any change in me, it was simply this queer
sensation of being dispersed. But I feel that, through this, I
did actually undergo a certain, more radical change. The
distinction between inner and outer became less defined for
me. Now, as I lay there on my back, swamped in the sound
of the downpour of rain incessantly streaming down outside, I sank deep into the actual sensation of those countless
raindrops falling into filthy water. When I reached the point
where I began to say to myself, "I'm raining outside," I
decided that this was a fine case of insanity, and I simply
ought to change hospitals.

Then one evening there was a soft knock on the door,
and there stood that superior of mine, like some ghost, in
the pale light of the rainy afternoon. This was the last person I was expecting to show up. No doubt he'd felt he too
had to come, since everyone else had. I felt rather disgrun-
tled at the idea that he'd come along like the rest to bandy
about a few pleasantries on the subject of my "heroic act."

But no sooner had he reached my bedside than he said, "What a terrible thing to happen!" He sat down on the chair beside the bed and murmured again, "Really, how terrible for you. . . . ," and he sank his head into his hands as though it were he himself that the accident had happened to. Even when that day of midsummer rain finally began to darken in the room, he still sat on in silence.

On Nakayama Hill

JUST AFTER MIDDAY ON the last Saturday of September, a young woman pushed her way hastily off the Sobu Line train just as it was about to leave Shimousa-Nakayama Station. The train was packed with students returning from school and people on their way to the racetrack one stop farther down the line at Nishi Funabashi, and some of those getting on were elbowed or trampled by the girl as she made her sudden last-minute dash out the door. After the doors had closed they stood glaring out at her through the glass, but the blue-jeans-clad young woman simply turned her back on the train and instead stood gazing up in apparent surprise and interest at the station name that hung from the ceiling, while one hand gently rubbed her lower back. When the train had left, she stepped lightly down the staircase now virtually empty of people. Though still young, she seemed close to thirty.

She had got on at Shinjuku. Lowering herself into a seat

in the corner of the still almost-empty carriage, at first she had sat gazing blankly at a headline announcing a plane crash in the magazine advertisement that hung from the ceiling, her face harsh with fatigue, until after a while her eyelids dropped. At Ichigaya she had roused herself, turned suddenly to glance toward the moat, and made as if to gather herself to disembark within the next few stops—but then she fell asleep again, arms folded and head lolling, and had proceeded to sleep right through until the train reached Shimousa-Nakayama, her eyelids occasionally flickering upward to reveal the whites of her eyes. She was momentarily delayed at the ticket gate while her fare was recalculated. When she finally stood looking out onto the square in front of the station, where a light rain was falling, her lusterless forehead was nevertheless suffused with a faint flush, perhaps from her forty-minute sleep in the train. The rain was not unexpected, for the clouds had hung low in the sky since early morning and the sunrise had been a ghastly red, so most people returning from the city were carrying umbrellas. She stood under the eaves, watching the umbrellas come and go, one hand still attentive to a place a little behind her hip bone. She could have been waiting for someone to come to meet her; but when the next train disgorged its passengers she set off among them, quickly stepping across the square, and entered the main street with its rows of shops opposite the station, her head unbent despite the rain.

As she proceeded, her pace became more casual, and she

ran a woman's professional eye over each shop as she passed, until she reached the Chiba Highway intersection. Here her interest seemed suddenly to flag, and she stopped and looked about her with an almost desolate expression, but when the lights changed she walked unhesitatingly across and went on. Coming to the tracks of the Keisei Line, she went over the level crossing, with her eyes on the platform of Keisei Nakayama Station that rose abruptly on her left, then passed through the big temple gate that straddled the road and walked on without pause up the long sloping street that led, flanked by old houses, toward the south gate of the temple Hokekyoji; she was stepping out with straight back now, no longer slightly hunched against the pain, seeming almost drawn on by the great gate up ahead of her.

The wet roadway was faintly pungent with the scent of magnolias, although neither flower nor tree was visible nearby. It may have been because of the recent summer heat or the unseasonably early onset of autumn, but from within this faint scent a sharp sour smell from time to time invaded her nostrils. It was reminiscent of the scent of a human armpit, which can suddenly somehow carry a certain sweetness within it. She was unable to decide whether this scent came from her own skin or had transferred itself from the skin of another.

Ahead of the girl, climbing slowly up the hill, was an old man. Despite the drizzle, he was using his unopened umbrella as a cane; the jacket was worn and old, the black shoes alone gleamed with newness. His white hair was close-cropped, and there was an earphone stuck in one ear. As he walked he lurched forward with each step, dragging his right leg, occasionally seeming about to halt, then heaving his feet into action again. A kind of repugnance was stirred in her by the sight of his exaggeratedly straining back, and she quickened her pace in order to pass him, but when she was quite close she found that the last three paces between them simply would not close. Watching him in some surprise then, she noticed that, although his pace was slowly growing more and more subdued, whenever she approached close enough for her presence behind him to be audible, he was hurried forward as if driven along from behind. His body seemed to quail at this undue haste, so she found herself slackening her stride to accommodate his.

It wasn't until they were passing through the temple gate at the top of the slope that she finally overtook him. The area beneath the roofed gate was paved with stones and gave off a scent of dry earth. Here the warm air at last brought a sense of longed-for relief to the girl, and she paused and ran her fingers through her dripping hair, momentarily forgetting the old man, who now stood a little apart from and level with her. As she stepped over the thick beam that formed the gate's threshold, her right hip ached dully and her inner thigh flinched. Her jeans pinched her miserably. This is the last time I'll do this, she found herself thinking. Then she realized that she had at last drawn level with the old man, who stepped across the beam of the threshold and then came to a halt.

He bent forward as if he might pitch face first onto the ground at any moment, his eyes staring emptily into space, and beckoned faintly to the girl with a forearm raised oddly high. Then, when she hesitated to approach him, he leaned weakly toward her; she was aware of a sudden hot metallic stench, a surprisingly stout hand gripped her right arm at the shoulder, and suddenly the whole weight of the man was hanging from her. She braced herself to take the weight, but her only thought as she continued to gaze out at the rain was, "Oh dear, he'll bruise my armpit."

"Now, now, nothing to worry about, no need to panic. I'm not going to eat you," the old man muttered, his eyes closed in apparent pain, while from his body flowed a faint thread of sound, a continuous and multitoned complexity of soft human voices.

"Is that a transistor radio?" she asked him after a moment, having at last divined the source of the sound. His half-closed eyes carried a strained smile.

"Jackpot time! This is just when it would happen, too. You wouldn't understand about this would you, dearie. Shiro and Shiro, two and four. The odds-on favorite Miksky's just about to take the lead from Shiro when they're pipped from behind by the other Shiro, wins by a neck. I guessed two four, you know. No fun listening to the radio and hearing it go just like you thought it would. Should have left home fifteen minutes earlier. Held up by a bit of a tiff with the family before I left. Still, could have made it if I'd caught the express straight to Higashi Nakayama instead of messing about at Takasago. What the hell, I thought, I'll go on the old local, and then I went and got off at Keisei Nakayama. Making it long for myself, silly old fool."

"How far is it to go back home, then?"

"No no, don't you see, I'm on my way to the races now."

"You mean there are horses in a place like this?"

"Where've you come from, dearie?"

"Kokubunji."

"On the Chuo Line. . . . You come to the races?"

"No, I was going to get off at Suidobashi, but I slept right through."

"Slept through, eh? So why are you walking about in a place like this then?"

"Well, where am I exactly?"

"Mercy me. You must have time on your hands."

"Yes."

"Right then, I'll take you to the races. You keep an old man company till they're done. It'll earn you points in heaven, dearie. Can I hang onto your shoulder while we walk?"

"Is there really a racetrack? But this is a temple."

"Sure sure, right up ahead."

So saying, the old man stepped jauntily off into the rain,

but despite the brave words he quickly began to totter. The sour scent of a bedridden invalid rose from him, and glancing at him she saw that from the neck down his back was soaked as if with sweat, so she tugged from his grip the umbrella he was using as a cane and put it up to shelter him, wound his arm over her to her left shoulder and supported his not inconsiderable weight with her right shoulder, so that the fearfully thin body was flattened close against her. The old man closed his eyes once more, a slight frown creasing his brow.

"Are you all right? Please try to bear up. I'll call someone as soon as we get to a house."

"No, no, on we go. It's straight ahead to the racetrack. We'll be in time for the seventh race."

The stone-paved road stretched straight ahead, unpeopled. Despite the long climb, they seemed to be in a valley whose walls rose high on either side. Temple buildings with deep shadowy interiors lined the road, and at the foot of their luxuriant growth of hedge the deep scarlet of withering nirvana flowers glowed at intervals through the dimness of the rain. At each step the old man's body grew heavier, as with sleep. After some time he suddenly said in a muffled voice, "Yoshiko, you've been sleeping with a man, haven't you, dearie?"

"Good lord no, what, in broad daylight!" She was astonished to hear the hysterical high-pitched cry, which seemed not to be her own. I won't answer for last night mind you, she murmured in her heart, and could almost see then her own features, with a wrinkle of disgust creasing the nose. Her back twisted suddenly, and a dark ache shot through her, feeling somehow like another's pain. The old man fell silent, and gave no sign of waiting for an answer. His quiet breath was as of one asleep. He's walking along a road somewhere in the arms of some girl called Yoshiko, without the least idea of where he is, she thought. And then she felt suddenly as if she were on her way home, saying to herself, "Well, I slept way past my stop, but nothing happened, did it?" as she waved this couple off, having simply handed over to this unknown Yoshiko the dazed old man. So thinking, she straightened herself, took a fresh hold on the old man, who had started to slip from her grasp, frowned at the umbrella's wild tilt, and went on, where now a five-storied pagoda loomed dimly ahead through the fog of rain. Even when they reached a point where teahouses lined the right side of the temple road, she marched firmly on without glancing in their direction.

"Oh, stop a minute, dearie. Sorry, I'll just take a rest here." At the old man's firm tone she turned to look at a teahouse near the end of the row, where the road turned a corner. From its eaves hung a grimy signboard advertising various traditional foods, small bamboo baskets by the door were heaped with taros and souvenir knickknacks, and beside these stood a middle-aged man and woman who seemed to be the teahouse owner and his wife, gazing with humor and without any sign of surprise at the old man clinging to the shoulder of the girl.

"What's this, Mr. Nonaka, you've come along with another beautiful nurse today have you? You're really on the mend these days, eh?"

"No, no, I've had it. Every time I come it's farther to the damn racetrack."

"Walking all the way every week like this—it's wonderful. Tomorrow's the last day before it moves on to Fuchu, though."

"Yes, no more at Nakayama till December now. Well, I won't be making it as far as here by then."

Grumbling and complaining, the old man left the girl's side; then, drawing himself up and adopting a lordly pose, he strolled toward the teahouse, throwing a glance of mock surprise at the girl who was following with open umbrella held above him, then turning to scold the owner.

"Now, now, don't you go talking so familiar about the young lady, calling her a nurse like that. I haven't learned her name yet, but she's saved my life. Up at the temple gate just now I staggered so bad on these poor old pins of mine, if she hadn't caught me from behind, I would have gone flat on my face and cracked my skull open if not worse. Right about now you'd have been hearing the ambulance siren and saying to each other happily, 'Sounds like the old chap's finally had it.' Well, I went and barked my shin, so she's lent me her shoulder to get me here."

And with this generous mixture of lies and truth, he stepped inside with an air of being quite at ease in the place, climbed up onto the tatami mat platform and settled himself cross-legged against one of the wall pillars; then, with his gaze fixed on some distant point beyond the eaves, he languidly beckoned the girl to join him.

The girl bowed her head beneath the umbrella to indicate that she was about to take her leave, but when she folded the umbrella and propped it by the door she suddenly looked so wretched and drenched that all three gazed at her, and as she stood hesitating the kindly wife took her by the arm and she found herself stepping in under the eaves.

The teahouse owner encouraged her to step up onto the tatami platform, but glancing over at the old man who sat there glaring at the racing form, his elbows planted on the low table, she was suddenly overwhelmed by his grandiose air, and instead perched herself precariously near the entrance and sat mopping her hair back from her forehead to her neck with a handkerchief.

"I'll warm up a bit of sake, shall I?" said the wife, looking worriedly at her pale wet face. This threw the girl into confusion again, but at that point she heard the old man behind her call out, "You've helped me once already, my dear, and I'm going to ask you another favor. For pity's sake."

She found herself at a loss whether to twist to the right or swivel round to the left to see him from where she sat, and when she had finally squirmed herself into position he was sitting with the racing paper lowered, gazing over at her.

"Dearie," he continued, slipping into his former tone with her, "you'd be the sort who doesn't get too confused in an unknown place, right?"

"I think I'd manage. I'm from the country originally, so in fact. . . ."

"Strong legs too, by the look of you."

"Well, yes, I'm not sure."

"Could you run somewhere for me now?"

"Run somewhere?"

As if to cover for her obviously dubious response, the old man straightened himself formally before the low table and drew a wallet from his pocket. He took out two ten-thousand-yen notes, slapping them onto the table, then gathered them up together with a couple of pieces of paper and thrust the bundle toward the girl's chest. She took them with a gesture that shielded her breasts, diffidently returned the money to the corner of the table, and lowered her eyes to the slips of paper.

"What's it now, just one o'clock. Ten minutes from the temple gate to here, eh? The gates open on race seven at twenty past, betting closes three minutes before. I want you to get to the track in fifteen minutes. There's two bits of paper there. The one marked 'one' you take to the nearest window as soon as you arrive and just push it through to them. Don't say a word. If you make a mistake, they'll put you right at the window. You'll get your betting slip when you pay, and you keep that safe. The race will start any moment. You watch it, just for future reference. Then go along to the advance betting window. You with me? The advance betting window. There's information booths here and there, so ask there. I've dropped the next race, so you've no need to hurry. Go to the window and just give them the second bit of paper, pay as you're told, and get your ticket. Then you can take your own time to come back here. I'll get them to have something warm waiting for you."

"Do you think I'll find the way?"

"No problem, all you do is turn right out the door and go along with the temple grounds on your right, and the road will lead you straight there. Some of the lads will be on their way there now, so just follow along behind someone who's in a hurry. You can't miss it. But maybe gambling bothers you?"

"No I don't mind about that, but what if I make some mistake?"

"Well, if you do then you do, and that can be fun too. Look, I may seem to be asking a lot of you, dearie, but I'm not just getting you to run an errand, you know. I don't know what you do, but I've got a fancy to put my luck in your hands today. Can you give me a little hour of your time? Just have a good look round, and while you're at it, place any bet you want. I'm not going to make it beyond here today by the looks of it. It's in your hands now. I've come this far in life under my own steam, after all."

As the old man's faint voice wheedled and pleaded, his eyes were shadowed with fatigue and limpid as a child's.

"No need to understand anything. Better not to know too much, really."

The girl averted her eyes from the old man and turned her frowning face to her knees, carefully folded the slips of paper, then got to her feet. Her somber look suggested that she was about to refuse with an apology, but instead she murmured meekly, "I'll be back later then," and walked with still downcast face toward the door. The teahouse owner came trotting over, seized the notes from the corner of the table and thrust them into her hand, took the slips of paper and quickly checked the numbers, then said, "There he goes again, he's got real taste has Mr. Nonaka, always goes for the unpopular ones." And he grinned at the old man, who was now looking tireder than ever, gave the girl directions all over again, and finally bowed low and said, "I do apologize."

"Be sure and watch a race, now," the old man called solicitously from behind him.

The wife handed her the umbrella with a friendly smile, then came out the door with her, and they stood for a while in the light rain, umbrellas tilted together, apparently deep in conversation. After a little while a faint smile appeared on the girl's face, and they both turned somewhat coyly and together cast a quick glance back into the shop.

In response the old man at the table nodded fondly toward them. There was a strange whiteness about his eyes.

FAR OFF TO THE LEFT A little pack of horses set off indistinctly and had soon lengthened into a straggling line, plunging on deeper into the distance, quite unrelated to the vast crowd of humans who peered out toward them from the stands. The rain appeared to be thickening, and along the line of hills beyond the horses a smoky spume began to rise from the tips of the pine forest.

She had not paused for breath since she left the teahouse, and her damp forehead still burned from the exertion. She had no memory of where or how she had walked to come here. Intending to follow along behind the fast-walking men, she had instead found herself passing them one after another. As she passed each one, the stench of his male body hung thick in the air about him, and she hurried her steps as if to evade it, searching ahead for the next human shape.

Arriving at the racetrack, she held out her piece of paper politely at one of the windows lined up beside the entrance and was told by the laughing women that this was the entry-ticket window. But they showed her the way to the double-bets booth and so saved her trouble in the end. She paid four thousand yen and received a slip stamped "two, five," and when she finally drew breath in the middle of the crowd, she was overcome by a sudden sensation akin to dizziness. Darkness closed in on the peripheries of her vision, and she staggered as she made her way somehow to a toilet, where she crouched, her body suddenly afire with its own urgency, whispering to itself shamelessly, "I've slept with a man I don't even like, and now it's done, oh, take me again." When she finally grew calm and opened the door again, a man with an emaciated face was just approaching; although this was clearly a ladies' rest room, the man's eyes filled with a startled fear when he saw the emerging female figure. She hastened out, and when she had climbed to the stand a loud buzzer sounded, followed by an announcement that betting had closed.

After the horses took off, a strange calm settled over everything. The colorful group of horses moved through the distance like a child's dream or a merry-go-round, and finally turned toward the stand. Yet they were still distant, somehow listless; she watched them, finding it difficult to believe they would ever manage to arrive, and as she watched she saw them begin to avalanche down together almost as if the ground beneath them had tilted, then suddenly their violent animal bodies were right below her eyes, and then as suddenly they had lunged on past, scattering, and were moving into the distance again, now yet more colorfully dreamlike.

"Shiragiku!" a man's voice cried close beside her, and she flinched. Her face burned with a strong flush again. In front of the teahouse a little earlier, as she was about to set off, the wife had leaned her face toward her under the umbrella and whispered, "The old man hasn't long to live, he's got cancer."

He knew of it, she went on to explain, and had decided that until he finally took to his bed the races should be his sole remaining pleasure, so during the months when the races were on at Nakayama he had been coming over from Horikiri every Saturday. His family was astonished, but let him go. Up until the spring, he had dropped in at the teahouse each evening on the way home from the races, then from around the end of March he had taken to calling in there for a rest before noon, before going on to the racetrack. He always got off at Keisei Nakayama and walked up the long slope, though it increased the distance he had to go. By the time the spring flowers were blooming in the temple grounds, he was placing his bets and immediately retreating to the teahouse, where he would ensconce himself in a corner in front of the television for the rest of the day. He never got through more than a small pot of sake. The spring races at Nakayama finished in mid-April, and in June they heard a rumor that he was in the hospital. In midsummer there was speculation at the teahouse that he wouldn't be able to come anymore. But when the races returned to Nakayama in September, there he was again. They were surprised to see how well he looked, but it turned out that it was all he could do to get as far as there. Someone had seen him squatting down to rest, halfway up the temple slope. Nevertheless, this was the fourth week he'd managed to make it. When he first arrived his face would be deathly pale, but when he went home again he was always in high spirits, whether he'd won or lost, and he tottered off down the slope with jaunty steps after the owner had seen him as far as the temple gate. These days he usually got a youngster from nearby to race his bicycle down to the track to place his bets for him, but this lad had gone in to Tokyo early today.

"He's a good man, and he's been a faithful customer, and this may be the last time he comes, so my husband was prepared to go to the track himself for him today, but Mr. Nonaka seems to have taken a fancy to you, so you'll do this for him won't you—for a man who'll soon be gone?" said the wife, turning to look back into the teahouse. The girl turned with her, and as she did so she was appalled to realize that she had reddened as if rather a different proposition had just been put to her. Her eyes met the old man's distant ones, and in her effort to calm her flush she felt the smile on her face grow yet more coy.

"Oh look, why don't you take the bike," said the wife as she turned to leave, but the girl brushed this suggestion aside and set off on foot. The brazenness of the image of her own form astride the saddle burned hot in her.

"Shiragiku! Shiragiku! Shiragiku!" the man was crying on and on, in a high constricted voice. He was an elderly man, standing three rows down and a little to one side of her. Her eyes unconsciously followed the direction in which his body was straining, and she found herself watching a horse still coming up on the right, alone behind the others.

It was galloping with its back miserably hunched, as if tucking its tail between its legs. It finally attached itself to the rear of the galloping group, was pushed out to the side, and seemed for a moment on the verge of dropping behind again as its legs flung along, but it clung on and eased slowly forward to the middle of the group, then seemed at last to be nearing exhaustion. "Shiragiku!" cried the man again, now almost weeping, and at his cry the nearby horses appeared momentarily to halt at the voice, the yellow cap alone plunging rapidly on into the distance, its color growing paler till it disappeared from sight among the farther group of horses up ahead. "Shiragiku! Shiragiku!" cried the voice, now quite hoarse with effort, more like a sob than a cry. The girl turned her back on the racetrack and went down the stairs.

How is a woman seen if she walks alone in such a place? Yet the men gathered here were themselves no ordinary men. With unwashed faces and unrinsed mouths, as if straight from their beds, they exuded a raw energy mixed with a shadowy tinge of exhaustion, and the eyes of each were fixed on some inner point. Even when they were simply walking about, the gaze was unblinking, and if an out-of-place woman like herself passed them, they gave her not a glance. The more absorbed this gaze, the more there seemed a kind of light kindled within it. Sometimes the fixed look would relax, and they would see nothing. They were like bewildered infants. She found herself imagining what might happen if those eyes one after another lifted vacantly from that on which they gazed and all turned as one toward her, and a faint shiver ran down her spine. She continued to push her way through the flow of people, sideways on to them and arms tight against her sides, and when her eyes fell on a person of her own sex sitting vacantly in an information booth, she found herself intrigued at the unusual sight as she approached her.

In a somewhat lisping voice, the young girl directed her with the patient care and gentle tones she would use with a lost child. She found her way easily to the betting window and without any hesitation took care of the business as instructed. The old man had told her she could now take her time to wander back to the teahouse. "But I won't get too upset if you simply disappear," he had informed her gravely. Maybe I'll just disappear then, the girl thought, giving a show of scratching her head as if in doubt as she left the betting window. Then she found herself wondering just where she was and, glancing around, was further surprised at the quietness all about her. So many people were gathered there, milling busily about, but the only sound that filled the air was that of their footsteps; the faint clamor of voices was distant. Lightly closing her eyes for a moment as she walked off, the sounds could almost be those of a far wind blowing through the dry leaves of a forest. Only the shadows of men thronged and jostled and moaned softly together. Though she walked with head down among them, none brushed her shoulders. A path seemed to open up of its own accord before her as she went. There was no sense that they were even aware she was a woman.

When she came to the line of booths, where business now was slack, she paused. "Two five," she murmured, and her body blushed strangely at the unfamiliar coarse sensation of her lips as she spoke. Ever since she had hurried down from the stand, she had been haunted time and again by a dark omenlike voice close to her ear, and each time had had a sudden vivid image of the old man's mouth. "But if it did win, he'd be so happy if I took the money back for him," she murmured back, and, frowning, she turned and went toward the window. There was a sudden flurry of footsteps approaching behind her; a man in his thirties attached himself to a neighboring window and, with a joyous expression dancing in the eyes beneath his glasses, thrust his ticket in with a forceful gesture that set his body writhing and shifting about with impatience as he waited. Belatedly, the girl timidly held out her ticket too and examined the expression of the woman who took it. Then she felt the commotion beside her cease and a gaze focus on the nape of her neck. She turned her head away to shield herself, and then there was a sudden hot breath at her ear and the man was saying, "You had two five.... Say, are you alone?" She had just been nervously preparing herself for what the woman might say to her, so she merely gave a brief nod, but this was a mistake, for the man stiffened and withdrew his face from hers. "No joke now, when the races are over I'll shake off my pals, and we can . . . " His voice came again, this time soft with suggestiveness.

Sunrise had been a ghastly red. She had managed to slip into her clothes while the man slept, and opened the curtains an inch or two to peer out. In the street, people were already hurrying to work, and even as she watched the red glow within the low-hanging clouds swelled and deepened, and with it the ache in her lower back, now thrust into jeans, grew heavier. Little by little she edged away from him. The man woke then, murmuring soft words, and suddenly lunged at her, his eyes bloodshot. In the faint light his face looked rigid, as if his teeth were still gritted from sleep.

The steep road seemed endless. . . . The man had pushed her down again, dragging her clothes down around her knees. When she drew her knees up miserably together and rejected him, antipathy seemed to rise in him, too, and she seized her chance when the strength of his grip relaxed, and hastily shuffled away from him on her knees. "I'll take everything off," she said, and went to the next room, then rapidly tidied herself and slipped out. Though it didn't look far, her anxious feet found the climb to the top of the hill a long one. Her back ached so much that she longed from moment to moment to simply crouch down. She limped on relentlessly, desperately repeating to herself the meaningless words "I'll limp all the way to you, so don't turn me down." She managed to telephone a girlfriend who worked in Suidobashi to say she was on her way, then slept in the train, but aside from that brief interlude she felt that she had ever since been climbing up that long hill, hour after hour. Her friend might well be worrying that she'd had an accident, she realized.

Watching the woman inside the booth counting and recounting a number of notes, she assumed that some would be put to one side, but instead they were all pushed out to her. The man beside her gave a low moan of surprise. There were seven ten-thousand-yen notes. She peered into the booth dubiously, but the woman just gave her a brief nod and said softly, "Take care going home, won't you," then glanced coldly at the man beside her, who stood motionless, grasping somewhat less than ten thousand yen. She put the money away and left the booth, and after she had gone a little way she turned; the man was still leaning against the counter, gazing after her in astonishment.

"I'll take this money and go to the man I love," she said to herself with a laugh as she opened her umbrella outside the racetrack entrance. Her body filled with cruel elation at the thought of actually leaving the old man behind and going to give herself to the man she loved, and her eyes sparkled. But since she had no idea how else to go, she merely retraced her way along the road she'd come. The rain had now become a downpour. After a while, a spring came into her stride, and she realized that she was now on the downward slope.

"TOO BAD ABOUT THIS rain, eh?"

"It's certainly done some raining this month."

Passing along the now darkened temple road in the ever denser rain, a man called in under the eaves to the teahouse owner's wife as he went past. After answering, she watched him go toward the temple gate a little way, then turned to the business of closing up shop.

"These race-goers are heading home early these days," the owner said to a last departing customer, stepping outside the teahouse with him and looking up at the dark sky.

"Not many dropped in today after the last race, did they? They're going off home without stopping for a drink. Come to the races, and go back sober," the customer agreed. Standing beside the owner, he put up his umbrella with a weary sigh at the rain, asking softly as he did so, "You going to give Mr. Nonaka a ride to the station this evening, then?"

"Yes, that's the plan. It looks like the girl doesn't have an umbrella either."

"Ah yes, the girl. I don't know what strange windfall brought her, but she's certainly given old Nonaka happy dreams today."

"Dreams is right. He was fast asleep when two five came in over the radio."

"Then she turns up when he wakes up again, and hands over seventy thousand or more, eh?"

"She looked so innocent when she came in the door there."

"And here's me, going all the way to the racetrack just to get myself drenched, and coming home the poorer for it like this."

"Well they say it pays to ask a woman."

"I just wish I had half his luck."

"Ah, you've got to devote yourself the way Mr. Nonaka does before you'll be favored by the bodhisattva like that."

"Yes indeed, he climbs all the way up that hill, even though he can't get to the track anymore, doesn't he."

"He does that. Well tomorrow's the last day at Naka-yama, eh? You coming tomorrow?"

"I'm afraid I've got a family memorial service. It looks like this rain will keep on, doesn't it?"

"The odds-on favorite is worried too, I can tell you."

"Well, rain makes for a poor track, that's for certain, but it's no fun for a memorial service either. And tomorrow's dear departed had no truck with the races, I can tell you."

The customer stepped off into the rain, and the owner set about clearing up the teahouse front with his wife, the customer's laughter still hovering at the corners of his eyes. In the teahouse, now empty of customers, the girl was sitting on a chair in a far corner, daintily picking her way through a big half-eaten dish of sushi, correct as a little girl on her best behavior. Half an hour earlier the old man had borrowed a blanket and curled up on the tatami floor, and he lay there motionless, his sleeping breath faintly audible.

"It's a special celebratory gift from Mr. Nonaka," the

owner had told her firmly, "so you must polish them all off, you're young after all, and when you've finished we'll wake him up," and she ate slowly, feeling that she must take her time to finish them all and so give the old man a good sleep. He'd been sleeping when she got back from the racetrack, propped cross-legged against a pillar with the radio blaring beside him, his form suddenly somehow shrunken and diminished. She spoke to him and placed the money, the betting slip, and the receipt in front of him, but he wore an anxious expression as he listened, unable at first quite to grasp the situation in the face of the sudden bewildering blare of reality that was breaking in on him. Then he picked up the slip and stared at it. "Ah, so I didn't buy for the eighth race. It gave me quite a turn when that dark horse snuck in like that," and with his next breath the joy began to grow in his face. He went on: "Well, dearie, this is wonderful!" and he slapped the notes and gazed up at her. "You'll stay a bit, won't you? If you go, I'll feel my luck has left me. Don't leave me lonely," he continued with imploring eyes. At this point the owner came over, and there followed a general happy fuss over the old man's good fortune. He's just like a baby who's woken from a nap, she thought with a fond smile.

When the next race came on the television, the old man moved to the table and sat her firmly down beside him. He ordered her some hot sake and added an order for the boiled taros that were displayed in little baskets at the shop front, with a promise that he'd get her something tasty to follow, and then sat there glued to the screen, assiduously topping off her sake with solicitous care, while an endless flow of spirited monologue poured forth. "Oopsy, how about that if you please, he'll pull away from them now." "What the hell's with that Futoshi? Stop, go, stop, go like that. Why doesn't he just disappear the hell out of there and be done with it!" She began by playing with the boiled taros politely, but then became intrigued by the way the skin slipped neatly off to reveal the white flesh, then discovered how luscious and sweet they tasted, and before she knew it she had dispatched the entire basket of them. Without a glance the old man ordered another, and slapped her on the back with a laugh, saying, "They're sexy things, aren't they, these local Nakayama taros."

From time to time he directed her to look at the screen, and told her to memorize the colors of the jockeys' caps. "Black and white, red and blue, okay? Yellow and green, marmalade and pink," he repeated, dividing them carefully into bite-sized pieces of information for her, then getting her to repeat them. It was enjoyable to follow stumblingly, naming the colors after him, and she took particular pleasure in the sensation of the word *marmalade* as she rolled it over lips and tongue, so she happily repeated the list for him over and over. Otherwise, he didn't explain to her anything of what he watched.

When the old man grew quiet again, she realized less than an hour had passed since he had begun to watch the television. The horses poured across her vision in seemingly overlapping waves. "It's already evening," she thought as she gazed at the rainy darkness of the racetrack.

"White's moving up on the inside. Give him a call, dearie," came the old man's voice, and she saw the white cap go swimming up to the lead like a little white ball flowing through the dark scene. "Pink's still in there—ah here's another. No, it looks like pink has it," he cried, his voice still gay; but then the horses passed the finishing post and the owner, who had been watching behind them, murmured as he turned to leave, "What? One eight, is it? Should have guessed as much," whereupon the old man turned his face slowly toward her and looked at her almost suspiciously, and she saw a thin mist clouding his slightly upturned eyes. He continued to gaze at her in silence.

"He said it was one eight," she told him timidly.

"It's one eight, no question of it, that's the one I'm placed on, the one you bought for me," replied the old man hollowly, then he turned his vacant gaze back to the screen.

He scarcely spoke again after that. When next the mud-splattered horses came around he merely watched them dully, apparently without interest, and while they were still jostling for position his hand reached casually over to the basket in front of her, took the last remaining taro, and slipped it straight into his mouth. He began to wipe his sticky hand on his jacket, so she stopped him and cleaned his fingers with a little hand towel, but his eyes never left the screen, and all he said was, "No good just thrashing along after him like that, man." Nevertheless, when the television broadcast ended he turned to the radio again, and called to the teahouse owner's wife, "I've met a lucky lady today. Let's all celebrate with some sushi, eh, make it for ten, that Yajima's bound to be along any minute pulling a long face at his luck."

"Well let's make that five—all right, six then," the wife replied, making her own decisions, and she scampered to the phone to put in the order.

When the sushi arrived, the old man watched as though pursuing some distant memory, as the large lacquer dish was carried gaily in through the door, which opened onto the dark temple road now busy with the hurrying umbrellas of the returning race-goers.

"Mr. Nonaka, did you pick eight eight for the last race?" asked the owner, to jolly him along.

"I did. Had it pegged," he replied nonchalantly.

"What a guy! How lucky can you get?" cried the owner in an astonished voice, but the old man paid him no attention and simply continued to gaze with apparent surprise and interest at the approaching sushi. Then old Yajima came bustling in out of the rain, and the five of them gathered at a table in a far corner away from the other customers and dug into their little feast together. . . .

She felt a strange uneasiness as she sat alone now at the lacquer dish and watched the sushi disappearing one by one.

The old men had sat happily chatting about past races they had known and scarcely reached for the sushi, so she found she had been encouraged to eat almost three people's portions herself. The more she ate, the more her appetite grew—along with a deep peace. Soothed by all the attention of being petted like a little girl by everyone, she now found her face had assumed an expression of almost childish innocence. "If I put down my chopsticks, the old man will wake up," she whispered to herself over and over.

"THANKS FOR ALL YOU'VE done today, dearie. You're off to meet a man now, eh?" the old man said to her in the car, the smell of sleep still thick about him.

She bit back the "yes" that was about to rise quite unbidden to her lips and instead asked in a small, hoarse voice, "Why do you say that?" as she gazed ahead through the fog of rain at the graveyard darkness that continually loomed toward her along the narrow winding road they were descending.

"Well, I just sensed it, that's all, watching you just now eating those sushi," the old man replied, in a voice now suddenly strong and robust. "And besides, I'll sleep sweeter tonight if I think of you throwing yourself into the arms of some man."

The motionless back of the teahouse owner registered nothing of the suggestive turn in the conversation. He simply continued to drive.

YOSHIKICHI FURUI was born in Tokyo in 1937. He received a master's degree in German Literature from Tokyo University in 1962 and taught German before beginning his career as a writer in 1970. His novel *Yoko* received the Akutagawa Prize in 1971, and since then his works have received numerous awards and prizes from the Japanese literary establishment, including the Tanizaki Prize, the Yomiuri Literary Prize, the Kawabata Yasunari Prize, and in 1997 the Mainichi Cultural Prize.

Translator MEREDITH MCKINNEY is a graduate of Australian National University and is a Ph.D. candidate specializing in medieval Japanese literature. A resident of Japan for twenty years, she translates classical and modern prose and poetry.

OTHER TITLES FROM STONE BRIDGE PRESS
IN THE ROCK SPRING COLLECTION OF JAPANESE LITERATURE

Death March on Mount Hakkoda by Jiro Nitta

Wind and Stone by Masaaki Tachihara

Still Life and Other Stories by Junzo Shono

Right under the big sky, I don't wear a hat by Hosai Ozaki

The Name of the Flower by Kuniko Mukoda

CONTEMPORARY JAPANESE WOMEN'S POETRY
A Long Rainy Season: Haiku and Tanka
Other Side River: Free Verse
edited by Leza Lowitz, Miyuki Aoyama, and Akemi Tomioka

Basho's Narrow Road: Spring and Autumn Passages
by Matsuo Basho, with commentary by Hiroaki Sato

Naked: Poems by Shuntaro Tanikawa

Hojoki by Kamo-no-Chomei

Milky Way Railroad by Kenji Miyazawa